THE

FORGOTTEN

Gods and Monsters applying for permanent residency in Canada

A collection of short stories

C.M.HINDMARSH

ISBN 978-1-7772346-0-7

ACKNOWLEDGEMENTS

Cover art image by LoganArt from Pixabay

Author photo by Angela Fama Photography

Author online:

www.cmhindmarshbooks.com

TABLE OF CONTENTS

SILVER 1

TEA ON A WINTER'S AFTERNOON 23

SIKU 37

THE TOLLING 51

THE CHOICE 77

THE LAKE 89

DOUBLE DOG DARE 113

AEGIR'S OFFERING 163

FRAGILE LITTLE THINGS 183

PROSPECTING 193

THE RECRUIT 219

MENAGERIE 233

GROUND ZERO 261

What you leave behind
is not what is engraved in stone monuments,
but what is woven into the lives of others.

Pericles

Katya sings along to Nickelback, which is currently blaring from the tinny car speakers. She peeks in the rear view mirror to see what her daughter is up to. Her daughter, Anika, smiles and coos along happily with her mother in a not bad but not yet harmonious harmony.

(But really - what did Chad Kruger expect?)

Katya and Anika make a good pair and it's obvious that they come from the same Germanic bloodline. Katya is lithe and blond and could easily replace Taylor Swift as the alt rights *(Nazi)* pin up girl. And Anika, though just a baby, is the spitting image of her mother. And spits she does. She spits up a mixture of spittle and baby food that is unfortunately from the green vegetable family.

And instead of getting angry or upset, Katya just laughs and asks, "Is it time for your exercises Regan?"

Katya swerves, a bit, over the median line and corrects herself but there is no danger of colliding with another car. She hasn't seen a soul since beginning their trek to Fort Resolution on desolate Highway 6. They're on their way to meet up with Katya's husband and Anika's father, Chris, who just recently scored a job as Chief Biologist working for the Dene. He will be doing ecological surveys of Great Slave Lake for some time to come and they decided to just pack up the car and surprise him.

"Looking good for Daddy, Babe!" Katya laughs.

Anika coos in the direction of a small grove of trees that seems to have sprouted from a large earthen mound. The mound is covered in what looks like soft grass and heather of all things.

"Good call!" Katya praises her daughter and turns the stiff wheel of her dilapidated white VW off the road and comes to a stop beside the mound.

"This will be our very own private rest stop. Where, as you may have guessed by now, we will rest." she smiles at Anika who smiles back in adoration of her loving mom.

"And clean up your demon puke!" she adds sarcastically.

Anika takes no notice. She is mesmerized by the swaying of the thin trees. They sway even though there's no breeze. Katya should have noticed such an anomaly! But she is currently focused on getting their rest stop supplies out of the car and wondering which of Anika's cutest shirts to get out to replace the current one – stained by demon puke. The problem is - they're all cute and hand-painted by her doting and highly creative godmother Tamara. A godmother who might be distressed at the current state of her work-of-art that Anika has also decorated.

Shirt changed, both fed – the girls decide to take a nap and Anika curls up on her Mom's chest. Katya stretches out and supports her back on a perfectly shaped tree. In mere seconds they are sound asleep.

Katya dreams about a grand soiree where all the guests are impossibly attractive. They're dressed in incredible garments of some natural fabric that pulse with deep rich color. Blues from Robin's egg to cerulean to Egyptian, reds with a much deeper hue than blood, the orangest oranges and many colors so breathtaking that words seem useless in describing them. A dance is underway and she is swept up in the music and the splendor. She floats from partner to partner, each more beautiful and graceful than the one before. It's a wonderful dream and Katya feels flushed with desire which quite frankly she hasn't felt in some time being a new mother. But underneath the glamour and the beauty she feels a foreboding! A feeling that all is not as it seems.

Anika dreams about the sweet rich milk that she used to suck from her mother's breasts and for some reason is not allowed to have anymore. But mostly she tries to remember all the things she knew before she decided to return as a baby. All the things she knew as a being of light are fading fast. So very fast and if she could only remember what she wanted to explore this time around - she could get right to it!

Katya and Anika, being somewhat empathically connected, like all babies and mothers are, begin to awaken when they hear a strange sound. It's not so much that they hear it as they feel it. Feel it in the ground and their bodies. It sounds like a dull pounding of the earth-- perhaps someone digging?
Katya's heavy lids lift slowly and she squints to try and clear her vision because something big, something quite huge is filling it. She sits up straight, which shakes Anika fully awake, and Katya worries she might fuss. But Anika is spell bound and her bright eyes drink in the sight of something she has never seen before. Katya, a woman of the world, has never seen such a sight either – well at least not in real life.
Pawing the earth, not two meters away from the girls, is a massive elk with an impossibly big rack of antlers. So big in fact that the elk's upright posture defies gravity! Seeing that the girls are awake and able to see him, the elk stops pawing and looks straight into the eyes of Katya and Anika.
The girls stare back!
The elk raises his massive head, crowned with his impressive points, snorts loudly, turns and trots a few paces down a well-worn path. He beckons the girls to follow him with a nod of his snout.
Katya looks at Anika and Anika looks at Katya. An empathic course of action is agreed upon and, with Anika cradled in her arms; they hurry off in

the opposite direction of the elk and in the direction and hopefully, safety, of their VW. Katya runs along as fast as she can with Anika bouncing up and down with her every step. Anika smiles, enjoying the modified horsey ride, and burps frequently as a result of the action. Internally, Katya makes note of this.

Next time baby fussy, take her for a run!

Out of breath and her muscles complaining about their misuse, Katya settles Anika in her car seat stands and stretches.

"Has it been that long since I've been up on the tissue?" Katya wonders aloud.

"Better get back up when we get home and work out the kinks," she adds.

Back on the road to Fort Resolution, Katya has forgotten all about the unbelievable elk. She checks on Anika by looking in the rear view mirror and sees that she is fast asleep and drooling on another priceless work-of-art from Tamara. She laughs and returns her attention to the road, turns around a long slow bend in the road and SLAMS ON THE BREAKS! Taking up most of both lanes - stands the hulking figure of the elk, head lowered and jagged antlers pointing straight at the girls and the puny VW. The tires, of the beat-up old VW, having seen better days, can no longer stop on a dime. Instead, the car slides to the right then the left. Smoke fills the air, and they finally comes to a stop so close to the tip of the nearest antler that it scratches the paint. As the smoke dissipates and the squeal of the tires is replaced by uneasy silence, it's Anika that utters the first word.

Okay, not a word really but a sound that in baby language means, *Freakin Cool! Much better than a horsey ride, mom!* .

Katya looks down at her hands, still holding tight to the sticky steering wheel, and marvels at how white her knuckles are. Not surprising as Katya has gripped it so tight, all the blood has drained away. Katya stares into the elk's eyes.

The elk stares back!

She tries the car horn and gives it a tentative toot. The elk doesn't move or flinch in any way. If it was possible for an elk to do - the elk would give Katya the stink eye!

"Should I go around him, baby?" Katya asks her daughter.

Anika doesn't make a peep but continues to stare at the magnificent creature in their way.

"Okay, I'll just edge forward as if it's a cow and maybe it will give way." Katya says aloud and not very convincingly.

She eases the VW to the right, ever so slowly, but the big beast doesn't move out of the way. It does move though and with unexpected speed lifts and raises it's massive antlers up and down onto the hood of the now trembling VW. The quiet is shattered with the crash of antler and metal scraping together. Katya stops and places her hands on her head in frustration. The noise from the antlers has upset Anika and she has decided to skip all the usual steps and goes straight into full-blooded wailing!

Katya looks back at Anika, a bit ashamed of herself for waiting this long to check on her.

What the hell was I thinking?

Katya engages the emergency brake, wriggles out of her seat belt and leans over into the back seat. She tries to soothe her daughter, as best as she can, with caresses and pats and sweet nothings but Anika is having none of it! In fact her screaming reaches new heights and goes all the way to eleven. Katya joins her daughter and starts to cry as she can appreciate her feeling of helplessness. Here they are, hundreds of kilometers from the nearest town. They have no hope of any resolution or rescue and there just happens to be a giant elk pinning their car to the middle of the highway! Katya and Anika gasp at the same moment as the giant snout of the giant elk fills the window right beside Anika and fogs the window. The enormous eye regards Anika with fondness and a touch of sadness and Katya would swear, much later, that the elk had a tear in it's eye. The elk takes one last longing look at Anika and a quick glance over to Katya and then bounds into the forest as gracefully as a gazelle or a white-tailed deer.

Anika and Katya stare into the forest for a long time, not saying anything and barely breathing. Their reverie is finally broken by the far-off and mournful cry of the elk.

Katya entertains Anika, as she drives down the empty highway, the magical elk a distant and fading memory. This time she sings along to Bruce Cockburn's ' Wondering where the lions are? ' She asks Anika where the lions are? Anika hides her eyes with her hands and laughs. Katya laughs too and in no time the girls have completely forgotten their encounter with the monstrous elk with the obscenely big antlers. Anika points out the front window and Katya looks in the direction she is pointing. A small town in the midst of some kind of celebration.

"Ohhhh!" Katya says excitedly, "I wonder what's going on?"

On one side of the highway, a group of kids is putting the finishing decorations on their old bikes and when Anika and Katya drive by, they all wave. Anika waves back while Katya's attention is on the road and someone dressed like a giant mosquito on an old motorcycle.

"Must be some kind of retro theme! Those bikes are from the seventies and eighties. A Cyberpunk gathering of some sort?" Katya asks out loud to herself and Anika but all she gets is a wet gurgling from her daughter.

"I don't remember a town on this route? Are we off course, Capitan!" Katya looks in the rear view mirror for an answer.

None comes. More gurgling.

"Shall we stop and check it out?" she asks Anika who rocks up and down in her car seat as an affirmative.

"Okay then. Let's find a side street to park our stead!" Katya states already turning onto a side street.

The girls stroll down the middle of the main drag, which has been blocked off with barricades and pylons. A hand-drawn sign informs them that this is ' Pine Point Days '.

"Huh? Must be a reference to a graphic novel." Katya nods to herself.

A group of teenage girls walks by. Some girls wear spandex, some high waist jeans with holes in the knees and they all have big hair.

Katya laughs, "Great costumes, girls!"

The girls skewer Katya with piercing silver eyes which soften as soon as they notice Anika. They fuss over the baby and make baby talk and cooing noises.

One girl, looking very much like Cyndi Lauper, asks, "So are you like a Viking or something? You look like Scandinavian!"

The rest of the girls nod.

"Ah, no. My ancestors are Germanic." Katya says proudly.

"Are you going to enter the cutest baby contest?" Cyndi Lauper lookalike asks, "You're baby is so freakin cute, I could just runaway with her!"

The others girls nod. Katya looks at the girls inquisitively trying to suss them out.

"Is there a prize?" Katya inquires.

"Uh, ya!" Cyndi Lauper lookalike exclaims, "A new freakin car!"

"Seriously?" Katya spits.

The girls nod.

Katya smiles down at Anika who smiles up at Katya, "Where do we sign up?"

The small town parade finishes, not with a bang, but a whimper as no one in small towns gives them much thought. This one consisted of the kids on their retro bikes, the mosquito motorcycle rider, a police car, a fire engine, and a convertible with the Mayor waving, like it was election eve, and some guy Katya thinks was a clown with a little yappy dog. Could have been some dude, down on his luck, who just happened to be walking on the same street, at the same time. Katya doesn't know if it's a trick of the light or it's some cosplay-themed contact lenses, but all the people in this hole in the wall have the same piercing silver eyes! Weird! And there aren't any old people.

The Mayor suddenly appears in front of Katya and Anika.

I'll kick you in the nards if you try and kiss my baby! Katya snarls in her inside voice.

"Well, you two are a long way from home!" the Mayor booms.

Katya looks him up and down, "Why would you say that?"

"You're from Sweden aren't you?" the Mayor asks politely, "You're Scandinavian features."

"German!" Katya frowns.

The Mayor continues, grinning at Anika, "I hope you're entering the cutest baby contest? The mine kicked in with a brand new car!"

Katya softens a bit, "We thought we just might."

The Mayor beams, "Excellent!" and whispers to Katya, "She's a shoe-in. I'm one of the judges!"

The Mayor winks at Anika with the disconcerting silver eyes.

Anika begins to fuss.

"There, there cutee! I bet everyone here wishes you were their very own!" the Mayor coos to Anika.

"Got to run, see you two at the contest.," the Mayor says as he flits away.

Katya stands off to the side with Anika, away from the festivities. She and Anika study the peculiar town folk as Tesla might have looked down on the citizen's of New York - bustling along the streets.

"What do you think, baby?" Katya asks Anika, "Should we stay for the car or get the hell out of Dodge?"

Anika answers, by rocking up and down, her physical expression for ' yes '.

Katya pulls her in close and lavishes kisses on Anika's head and face. Anika playful spits them away, laughing.

"I agree, let's get back in the car and go see Daddy," Katya confirms with a smile and longing sigh.

"All set?" Katya glances back at Anika, securely fastened and snug in her baby seat.

Anika rocks up and down.

"Alright, let's roll!" Katya nods as she turns over the engine.

But the engine doesn't turn over. In fact, nothing happens, not even the high-pitched whirr of the starter. Unperturbed, Katya tries again and the engine, that usually purrs into life in milliseconds and quite efficiently – because it's German, back fires once and only once.

"What the hell?" Katya queries as she slams the palms of her hands into the sticky steering wheel.

Katya looks back at Anika who blows a spittle bubble which pops loudly in the silence.

"You said it, kiddo!" Katya sighs.

"I guess we try our luck at the contest?" Katya glares at the dial indicating zero rpm's.

Katya strides into the convenience store setting off the door camel bell and smiles.

"These cosplayers don't miss a beat!" she tells Anika who decided that she needed a nap and hangs limply from Katya' s grey hemp-wrap carrier.

Katya scans the store but frowns when she doesn't see what she needs. She catches the eye of the sixteen-year-old kid behind the counter whose face is badly pockmarked. He looks up from the slurpee, he seems attached too, with an air of annoyance - probably pissed off as he's missing the festivities!

"Where' the ATM?" Katya inquires politely.

"What?" the slurper replies.

"The ATM! The money machine?" Katya specifies.

"What the hell is an ATM?" he frowns, "I don't know what goes on in Norway, but I never heard of such a thing. Here visiting?" the slurper brightens up having never met anyone from Scandinavia.

Katya rolls her eyes, "What about cash back? I'll buy something!"

The slurper wrinkles his brow, "Depends on what you give me. You don't get cash back if you give me exact change."

Katya stares at the teenager, in disbelief, and considers asking another question but stops herself.

"Sure is a cute baby! You should enter the contest." he smiles.

Katya high-tails it out of the store and on to the street. She sighs seemingly out of options. She looks up and down the street and observes that there aren't many other stores and they all seem closed for the holiday.

"Maybe I should call Chris." she ponders knowing it would ruin the surprise.

Anika rocks up and down, now wide-awake.

"Should we call daddy?" she asks her baby.

Anika rocks with more enthusiasm and goos for good measure.

Katya fishes out her Iphone, looks at its face and her own face falls.

"No service. Why re we not surprised, baby!" Katya posits.

Anika spits drool in solidarity.

The entire town seems to be crowded around the makeshift wooden stage in the middle of the main street.

I wonder where all the old people are? Katya ponders internally.

Standing on the platform is the Mayor, grinning from ear to ear. Four other mothers stand stoically beside him - their babies lying in ancient rusting and paint-peeled strollers. Katya and Anika, stand off to one side feeling a bit uneasy. The Mayor, who Katya has decided is a sleaze ball, winks at her every time he catches her eye. This is also disconcerting as the eye he winks is that eerie silver color. The other mothers on the platform have the same eyes! Katya wonders if the sleaze ball has impregnated the entire town? Maybe this isn't a cosplay event. Maybe it's a rather messed up family re-union! The convenience store kid sure seemed inbred!

The Mayor taps the microphone and then spreads his arms wide.

"Thank you all for making Pine Point Days a wonderful success!" he beams.

Katya thinks that, at this point, the assembled crowd should clap for the holiday and for themselves. But they just stand stock still, smiling an eerie smile and seemingly staring at Anika.

(How does one describe an eerie smile?)

(Well, imagine the smile on the Picton brothers faces as they hosted yet another successful shindig in their barn. And knowing what murderous acts they had performed in that very barn and so far - they were getting away with it!)

Katya and Anika share one of their telepathic moments and agree that they should make a run for it. But just as they turn to run off the back of the stage, even more silver-eyed people press in and block their escape route.

The Mayor, who has never stopped addressing the crowd, continues, "So we will judge the cutest baby contest based on your applause. Let's get started."

The Mayor points to the mother and baby farthest away from Katya and Anika and the crowd stands stock still and smiles at Anika. All the mothers, in the contest, smile and marvel at Anika. It's as if they don't fancy or care about their own chances.

Katya shuffles her feet nervously and Anika fusses. The Mayor points to the other three mothers and their babies and the crowd reacts in the same way – they don't react at all. And then the Mayor holds up his slender pointing finger, holds it up for all the crowd to see. And like a seasoned actor he holds that moment, letting the suspense build and build. Some of the previously stock still silver-eyed locals actually twitch a little – being brought to the precipice but left teetering on the edge.

Katya and Anika squeeze their eyes shut unable to stand the sight of the Mayor and his brood.

Katya imagines the sound of a drum-roll but not a drum-roll for happy occasions. She imagines the kind soldier's would play just before the guillotine fell.

The crowd roars their approval! The Mayor must be pointing at Anika - right this second. Katya, her eyes still closed, grimaces at the thought. Anika has skipped the ' quietly beginning to cry phase ' and gone directly to full on bawling and screaming at the top of her lungs. Katya's eyes snap open and she relaxes a little realizing that Anika is just reacting to the noise and is not in danger. Poor baby Anika tries to bury her tiny head in the folds of the baby carrier and under Katya's breasts. She would happily return to the womb if only to get away from the silver-eyed whoops and cheers.

The Mayor uses his hands to try and silence the crowd, "Thank you all for participating." he motions to the losing mother's and babies, "The crowd has spoken and what a deserving winner! Let the crowd have a good look, mom, just for a minute. I know they can be overwhelming!"

The Mayor smiles, pleadingly, at Katya, who begrudgingly nods, and begins to untangle Anika - who is frantically searching for her long-lost umbilical cord.

"Come on honey, just for a quick minute and then we'll get in our new car and go see Daddy!" Katya coaxes and strokes, rubs and kisses the most important thing in her entire world.

Anika turns down her rebellion, against a loud and cruel world, from eleven to a simmering five.

"Thanks baby! I can't ask for anything more than that." Katya showers Anika with more kisses.

Anika allows Katya to disentangle her and remove her from the carrier. Katya holds her out in front of her for all the silver-eyed people to see.

Collectively they smile and sigh, "Awwwwww!"

Even Katya, softens a little, and a tiny smile begins to crack on her Scandinavian face!

(Oops! German face!)

The Mayor, being quite a bit taller than all of his potentially inbred town-folk, reaches over and snatches baby Anika right out of Katya's hands. He then lifts the baby high in the air for all to admire. Katya flies at the Mayor, a mother cougar keen on ripping his silver-colored eyes out. One, two, three silver-eyed townies zigzag in front of and between Katya and the Mayor - blocking any attack. Katya, undeterred, punches and kicks and tries to scratch them out of the way. The Mayor's defensive trio stand stock-still with their arms folded in front of them. They just smile and deflect her blows seemingly unfazed by the attack.

The Mayor catches her eye and winks then turns back to the mic, "Let's feast our eyes on the cutest baby in Pine Point and then we can return her to her mother. In the meantime, why don't you have a look at your BRAND NEW CAR!"

Just in front of the makeshift stage, the silver-eyed locals part. The space reveals a brand new gleaming red Pontiac Firebird with two thick black stripes adorning the hood. Katya is so taken off guard that she momentarily forgets about Anika and the bizarre town and festival that she is now a big part of.

"What the hell?" is all Katya can manage and laughs when she thinks about the look on Chris' face when she rumbles up the drive with Anika in the back seat.

Anika!

Katya spins around, trying to spy her daughter, and lets out a deep breath she hadn't realized she was holding in. She sees her beautiful daughter happily cooing at the Mayor and grabbing and twisting the Mayors thin and pointy nose.

That's odd! Katya ponders inside her head; *She always fusses with strangers at first.*

The Mayor doesn't seem to mind the nose twisting as he laughs along with the crowd. Anika's nose twisting might be the cutest thing the Northwest Territories has ever seen!

Catching Katya's eye again, the Mayor winks then turns back to the crowd, "Time to give her back to mom who has been such a great sport!"

The crowd jeers and the Mayor hands the baby back to Katya who holds her close. Anika stops cooing and spitting. She yawns and falls asleep.

As Katya wraps the baby up in the carrier again, she thinks to herself, *Weird!* but doesn't dwell on the odd behavior, just happy to have her baby back.

The assembled crowd of silver-eyed people has returned to their stock-still positions and smile as they gaze fondly upon the Mayor, hands on both sides of the podium, smiling and leaning into the mic.

"And now to complete the bargain!" The Mayor proclaims in a rather serious tone.

He fishes car keys out of his back pocket and hands them to Katya. Katya holds them in her hand, palm up and studies them.

I never win anything! she thinks to herself, *Maybe our luck is changing!*

And yet another part of Katya's brain or perhaps her gut, wonders if she is missing something? Has she forgotten something? Is this all too easy?

Then the ' flashy new things ' part of her brain takes back control and says, *A new free car!*

The keys, in Katya's hands, mesmerize her. They seem to flash the daylight in an odd but still rhythmic pattern. The silver-eyed people begin to sing. They sing a song Katya has heard before but she can't remember just where it was and are the glittering keys and the singing in synch with one another?

An odd mournful call from far away.

That's a strange sound, Katya thinks as she continues to stare at the keys. *I wonder where the crowd has gone; it's become awfully quiet.*

Another mournful cry and this time much closer.

"Poor creature! Sounds so sad and despondent!" Katya sighs.

Katya begins to feel annoyed when she hears another strange sound. The new sound begins to draw her attention away from the glittering keys. It's not so much that she hears it –it's more like she feels it. Feels it in the ground and her body. It sounds like a dull pounding of the earth, perhaps someone digging?

Katya's heavy head turns away from her treasured keys begrudgingly. She squints to try and clear her vision because something big, something quite huge, is filling it up. She sits up straight shaking Anika fully awake and Katya worries that the baby might fuss. But Anika just stares into space not concerned in the least. Katya returns her more focused gaze back to the source of the noises.

Pawing the earth, not two meters away from the girls, is a massive elk with an impossibly big rack of antlers. So big in fact, the elk shouldn't be able to hold them up! The elk stops pawing and looks straight into the eyes of Katya and then at Anika.

Anika, it would seem, is indifferent to the giant beastie and looks out the window in the opposite direction. This provokes a response from the massive elk who slowly clomps over to Anika's side of the car. The elk pushes it's huge face as close to the window as possible and stares into Anika's eyes. Katya now fully awake sits stock-still, frozen to the spot and not wanting any sudden move to agitate the elk - mere centimeters away from her beautiful baby. The elks huge orbish-eye waters. Waters as if it was crying and bellows out a long and soul-wrenching cry that makes the VW vibrate.

So mournful is the elk's cry that Katya's own tears begin to well and her lips begin to quiver.

The elk lifts it's huge head and shakes it from side to side then turns and trudges away in the same direction that it first appeared. It stops, turns back to look over its shoulder and locks eyes with Katya. It shakes it giant head from side to side once more. The elk cries, this time more softly and edged with despair. The hulking beast turns and clomps away, along a well-worn path, into the forest.

Katya notices the white car hood as she looks out the front windshield.

Supposed to be red with black stripes! she thinks.

She looks down at her hands, knuckles white and still griping the sticky steering wheel of her beat up VW. She looks back in the rearview mirror at Anika - still blankly staring out the window. She reaches out telepathically to Anika to share a re-assuring feeling. But the familiar spiritual energetic bond between a mother and baby is seemingly not there anymore.

"Anika?" Katya whispers, not wanting the growing panic spreading through her to affect the evenness of her voice.

Anika doesn't react.

"ANIKA!" Katya yells, to hell with caution!

Still nothing! Not even a wet gurgle or a spit-bubble.

Katya scrambles out of the drivers seat, out her door and wrenches open the rusty one beside her daughter.

I just need to touch her and hold her and shower her with sweet kisses! Katya reassures herself as she reaches in to unstrap Anika from her carseat.

But Anika is not there.

Katya stops mid-reach and all her life-giving breath escapes in a hiss.

In Anika's place is a rather large chunk of red leaf-colored clay in a rudimentary suggested and grotesque shape of a human baby. A baby devoid of any semblance of life.

Katya falls to her knees, her hands still outstretched and still ready to embrace her daughter. Rivulets of tears meander down her face and stain her jeans. Some drops roll off and onto the dusty ground - exploding in little clouds. Katya tries to say something. Her mouth seems to be trying to form the words but her vocal chords can only produce, what someone from the old country might describe as keening.

The Mayor's words burrow into Katya's left ear and then out through her right, "And now to complete the bargain!"

Katya shakes her head from side to side. A sign all creatures recognize as ' no '.

She shakes her head slowly, then building more frequency and intensity. From far, far away – she barely hears the mourning cry of the elk.

A cry she now understands.

The End

TEA, ON A WINTER'S AFTERNOON

William sits at, his very impressive, computer array in the middle of a winter weekday afternoon in the William Whyte neighborhood of Winnipeg. The blinds have been closed and the lights turned off.

William is sixteen, five-foot-nine and seventy kilos with thick black shoulder length hair. His mother would call him handsome but anyone else would say gangly and okay looking. He believes he's all alone in the house, which is probably a good thing. He sits, naked, in front of his thirty-two inch HD main video monitor and watches a slideshow. The images, on his self-created slideshow, are of Queen Daenerys Targaryen scantily clad and sometimes nude. And since William is sixteen, this is his third masturbatory extravaganza of the day and his penis is raw and quite sore looking.

(But did that ever stop a sixteen-year-old boy swimming in hormones?)

He's almost at the point of no return. This is unfortunate as William's mother has just unexpectedly arrived home early and has just shuffled in the front door.

Even more unfortunate for William, the sixteen-year-old compulsive masturbator, is the fact that he has his noise rejecting headphones on and he's listening to ' Tommy Gun ' by The Clash.

William's mother drops her purse and slumps down onto the Ikea wooden bench underneath the coat pegs and sighs. Not the sigh of relief but the sigh of hopeless incomprehension and the crushing weight of terminal illness. William's mother has lost a ridiculous amount of weight! Kilos and kilos of insulating blubber. Kilos and kilos of insulating blubber she really couldn't afford to lose because it's the middle of winter in Winnipeg. William's mother has collapsed onto the wooden bench to remove her extremely warm, but decidedly ugly. snowmobile boots. Neither William, currently stroking in his darkened bedroom, or William's Mother owns a snowmobile. It's a truly Canadian thing. It's like dressing up as an urban lumber Jack, never having touched an axe but having seen one online on a hardware store website.

Poor William's mother hardly has the strength to remove her strictly utilitarian snowmobile boots and she frequently takes little breaks to conserve her dwindling energy reserves.

William, on the other hand, who really only has one other hand available, is full of energy! So much energy, in fact, that some of it is already leaking out. William is close and even at the young age of sixteen; he has mastered the timing of his orgasms and therefore stops his pumping all together. At this moment, a speck of dust settling onto his red and puffy member would be enough to facilitate an out of body experience! So William begins to breath deeply from his diaphragm.

William's mother, finally unburdened from her survival gear, stands dizzily and uses her frail hands to support herself against the wall. Sensing that vertigo has passed, she shuffles along the hallway - like a blind woman - in unfamiliar surroundings.

Meanwhile, William, who has been practicing his kegel exercises, proudly moves his erection from side to side and up and down without using his hands. He's having such a good time - he can't help but giggle. Which in turn puts a smile on William's mother's sallow face, as she is a mere step from the open door of William's house of masturbation.

On the video monitor, Deanery's Targaryen is completely naked and astride her favorite dragon. Drogon. and looking over her shoulder seductively. This is the shot William has been keeping in reserve, just for the right moment.

(This is, as they say, the money shot!)

Coincidentally, *(What are the chances?),* William's mother has reached the open doorway. She pauses to steady herself, whilst leaning on the frame. From her point of view, all that William's mother can see is the back of William's head and a bit of dragon on the monitor.

She smiles and chuckles to herself, *Must be a video game.*

At that exact moment, William rocks back in his chair, eyes clamped shut and yells at the top of his lungs, "DRACARYS!"

In scientific terms, every action has a reaction,

Just as William drenched Daenerys Targaryen, Drogon and his Star Wars drapes with his sixteen-year-old splodge, The Clash finished singing ' Safe European Home '. This allowed William to hear the deep intake of breath from his mother. Having spent himself so spectacularly, William could open his eyes. Open his eyes and watch his ailing Mother fall to the floor in a dead faint. And since the song had finished, hear her wisp-like form hit the floor with a soft thump.

(Now, I'm sure we all have a sympathetic idea of how William felt seeing his fragile mother faint at the spectacle of her sixteen-year-old son extinguishing his very expensive video monitor.)

(But what about his mother?)

What thoughts raced through her mind just as her brain took complete control and said, *Okay, that's it! I'm shutting you down.*

Did she think, Oh, thank God he's not gay!

Or, *Does he have a thing for animals?*

Or, *That's a lot of cum!*

Or, *This is going to cost me a bundle in therapy.*

Or, *Puberty already?*

Or, *I blame his father!*

It could have been any of the above options really. But it wasn't.

Poor William's sickly mother scornfully thought, *If he thinks I'm going to clean that up – he's got another thing coming!*

William has just finished arranging his mother, in her bed, when he hears a very persistent and curt knocking at the front door.

"Now what?" he whispers not wanting to disturb his unconscious mother.

He lopes to the front door, curious and annoyed at the intrusion. William yanks open the door and finds two middle-aged women. They look very tired and laden down with files, clipboards and purses.

William, being a teenager and using a language common to teenagers all over the world says, "YA?"

The short and dumpy one flashes a wining and practiced smile. She's obviously the good cop in this tag team scenario.

She coos, "William?"

William challenges, "Who's asking?"

The taller birdlike woman screeches into his face, "Social Services! We've been called in to investigate your truancy. Numerous calls and emails have been made to your mother, apparently ignored."

William glares at her, imagining her nest mates - pushing her out of the nest.

"She's quite ill and I'm taking care of her," William spits defiantly.

The dumpy one looks genuinely concerned and about to cry. She's good!

"Oh, poor dear! So sorry to hear that. I'm Mrs., Puden and this is Tara." says Mrs. Pudin.

Tara dactyl or Tara me another asshole! William jokes in his head.

Mrs. Podin charms, "We need to make sure everything is okay at home and we'd like you to invite us in for a short visit and look round."

Tara snorts and pushes past William, "We don't need your permission!"

Mrs. Pudin follows Tara in and, as she waddles past William, she whispers, "She's a bit of a grump!!" and winks at William conspiratorially.

William lingers on the porch, soaking in the gloomy day. His eyes, normally a nice shade of green, transform into red and begin to glow like the coals of a forgotten fire re-invigorated by a slight breeze. William's extraordinarily long tongue lolls out and hangs like a dead snake from his lips. Heavy black clouds rumble in, looking like they mean business. William's fiery eyes fade back to green and he grins, sucks in his tongue, strolls back into the house, closes and locks the door.

William gestures to the living room and couch, "Since this is an official visit, I suppose I should offer you tea. I'll be right back."

Tara, "I prefer coffee."

William is already striding to the kitchen, "Tea! Will be ready shortly."

The muffled voice of William's mother calls out as William passes her door.

"Who's that?"

William throws her a dismissive hand gesture, "Social services. Stay in bed. I can handle them."

William busies himself making tea and fantasizes about riding the Targaryan girl.

He carries the tea back to the living room. Although only sixteen, William has prepared a proper tea service with milk and honey and delicate teacups and saucers.

The tea, Russian Caravan, is loose leaf, naturally black and smoky. Not too many people, but William and his mother, appreciate the rich smoky nature of this black tea. A fact that, William hopes, will encourage puddin pop and Tara dactyl to leave as soon as possible. Otherwise, they'll be forced to stay with the approaching storm. Forced to wait out the storm all alone and isolated with William and his Mother.

As William passes his mother's door he yells, "WANT TEA MOM?"

She feebly replies, "No thanks honey. Do we have any raw meat? Nice and bloody?"

William sighs, "No, sorry Mom."

His mother sighs then goes quiet.

William sets the tea service down, on the marked and worn Ikea coffee table, and pours. Mrs. Pudin is obviously impressed and even jots down a note on her clipboard. Tara, on the other hand, is disappointed there's no coffee and William wonders if she'll use her dainty teacup as a spittoon?

Tara flaps her leathery wings and leans forward, "Why is your mother home in the middle of the afternoon?"

William makes her wait. He fixes a cup for himself, sits across from the social workers, closes his eyes and savors the aroma of the tea. He takes a long slow sip, opens his eyes and glares at Tara.

"She's quite ill and most of the time – bed ridden."

(Pens fly over clipboards!)

Mrs. Pudin's syrupy voice makes the jar of honey blush, "Oh dear oh dear, what's the matter?"

William adopts the calloused, mature, official but clueless tone of a physician, "Wendigo psychosis!"

Mrs. Pudin gasps. Tara simultaneously spits-out her Russian Caravan and blows a raspberry! *(Which is quite an accomplishment)*

She spits again, "Get real!".

Mrs. Pudin's mouth still hangs open in stunned silence.

William imagines filling it up with Ping-Pong balls.

William confidently continues, "I assure you that Wendigo psychosis is a real disease and is not rare by any means. In our fair province of Manitoba, it's quite common."

Tara snatches up her iPhone and Google's.

(Imagine a pterodactyl trying to use a cell phone!)

Mrs. Pudin recovers herself, "Well, what are the symptoms?"

William leans forward and lowers his voice an octave, "An intense craving for human flesh,"

Mrs. Pudin covers her heart with her pudgy hands and Tara just snarls.

William continues undeterred, "And a fear of becoming a cannibal. I hope her craving isn't too strong today!"

Just then a growling moan escapes from William's mothers bedroom

The social workers jump in fright and spill their tea.

As they recover themselves, William wonders if he can get to the john and rub one out in two minutes or less? He thinks he can.

William is torn back from his masturbatory musings by a question from Tara.

"No one else to look after her?"

William looks her square in the eye, "Nope! Dad's been missing since two thousand ten and presumed dead."

Mrs. Pudin, "Oh my, what happened?"

William. "An avalanche near Dauphin."

Mrs. Pudin, "How awful!"

William shrugs, "Not really. What do you expect driving snowmobiles through avalanche zones?"

Tara, "Were you close?"

William, "No, he was a mean son of a bitch."

"WILLIAM!" roars William's mother from her convalescing bed.

William waves her away.

Tara, still annoyed there's no coffee, presses on, "And has your mother acted upon her cravings?"

William is flabbergasted for three milliseconds then recovers quickly, "Far be it from me to spill family secrets, but she is partial to lean cuts of meat!"

Mrs. Pudin's eyes grow wider as Tara hugs herself, showing a small chink in her confidence armor. William smiles slyly and picks up the teapot to pour himself more tea, only to find the teapot empty.

He looks at Mrs. Pudin's empty cup and smiles, "You like the Russian Caravan huh?"

Mrs. Pudin blushes, "It's delicious and I'm usually a ' Red Rose' kind of gal!"

Big surprise there! William laughs in his own head.

"Be right back "

William strides toward the kitchen, and puts the kettle on. A real copper kettle and not some modern abomination made of plastic with an element inside. But proper tea etiquette is far from William's testosterone addled mind. He's already dropped his drawers ready to spew load number four into a wad of toilet paper.

William's mother, knowing full well what her insatiable son William is up to, lurches out her bedroom and down the hallway to the living room - using the walls for support.

In the living room, Tara and Mrs. Pudin compare notes and observations.

Mrs. Pudin clucks, "Well, there is certainly room for leniency! What a series of tragic events."

Tara is nonplussed and looks like she just sucked on a lemon, "Sounds convoluted and I don't buy it! Wendigo psychosis? Please!"

An ugly crease appears on her face as if she is in excruciating pain - her version of a smile.

She continues, "I'll give the kid credit thought. It's creative!"

Suddenly, William's mother darkens the doorway. Her disheveled tattered nightgown barely clings to her jaundiced and emaciated frame. Her eyes are sunken dark orbs, her tongue lolls out and a string of drool stretches to the floor.

The horrific sight of William's mother results in three reactions.

First, Mrs. Pudin screams at the top of her lungs but she's so frightened no sound comes out. Second, Tara forsakes her ' too cool ' confident demeanor and back-peddles over the couch to the nearest corner, in which she cowers. Thirdly, Mrs. Pudin pisses herself! Fortunately, she had already donned a pair of adult diapers, first thing that morning. Not because Mrs. Pudin is incontinent, but because Mr. Pudin has a rather peculiar fetish. And last but not least, *(and yes it's technically number four)*, Mrs. Pudin faints. She falls back into the soft, warn-out, couch cushion.

William's mother, very undead-like, shuffles toward the roly-poly Mrs. Pudin. As she closes the distance, the hungry expression on her face intensifies. And the drool attached to her dark maw reaches to the floor like a spider building a web.

Tara, for some reason still cradling her un-spilled tea, showers William's mother and Mrs. Pudin with tepid Russian Caravan!

(Well, really what else does one do with tepid tea that one didn't want in the first place? Unfortunately, as a Wendigo repellent, it is highly ineffective!)

Realizing her error, though she would never admit it, Tara fires the dainty cup at the slavering William's mother.

(A well-aimed teacup, dainty or not, traveling at high velocity could cause appreciable damage to the nose, mouth or temple. Imagine the logistics of a pterodactyl throwing a dainty teacup!)

The teacup in question missed its mark. It did however connect with Mrs. Pudin's head. This was unfortunate as at that precise moment, Mrs. Pudin, was regaining consciousness from her fainting spell. Whether Mrs. Pudin upon awakening could have saved the day, will remain a mystery.

Being a dainty teacup, it smashed quite loudly into a million pieces upon hitting the floor. William's flesh-craving mother paid the shards no notice.

William, many rooms away and attempting a new masturbation record, did notice.

So close. So Goddamn close! William thought, as he raced down the hallway, his face flushed from other activities.

Bursting into the living room, he gasped at the sight of his drooling mother looming over Mrs. Pudin's inert and dumpy form. His unlaced Converse high-tops make contact with the lake of saliva his Mother is still adding too. As his feet ascend to the heavens, and his head descends toward the floor, he glances into the corner where Tara still cowers.

Not so tough after... is all his brain can muster before his skull and the scuffed hardwood floor - merge into something new.

The very same brain has decided that he is indeed worthy of an extra dose of DMT to shield him from the terrific bolt of pain that should be blinding him and taking his breath away.

(What a sight!)

William splayed out and sticking to his Mother's gooey mouth secretions.

Tara cowering in the corner and muttering to herself. William's mother just about to consume Mrs. Pudin - recently knocked out by her cowering co-worker.

But instead of tearing off strips of Mrs. Pudin's skin with her razor sharp teeth, William's mother slaps Mrs. Pudin over and over again. Tara stops her muttering and stands up tall to get a better view of this unforeseen change in the action.

William's mothers slappy onslaught has brought Mrs. Pudin to the brink of consciousness.

Mrs. Pudin begins to moan and form rudimentary words and at the same time – William does the same, still swimming in his mother's spittle. Mrs. Pudin opens her eyes and the first thing she sees is William's mother looming over her and she faints.

(Again!)

Meanwhile, William is conscious but still quite groggy and up on his elbows.

William's mother growls, deep down, in her torso and changes her focus to Tara. She lurches along the couch, bony arms outstretched for a macabre hug.

Tara raises her hands to defend herself and begins some very undignified pleading, "No. No. Please don't hurt me!"

William's mother closes the distance. Tara closes her eyes and waits hopelessly for William's mother to flay and devour her. And she waits, and she waits, and she waits but no claws rake her flesh. No fangs puncture her skin. Not even a drop of saliva sprays her. Tara opens her eyes to find William's mother teetering in front of her and looking quite forlorn. Like an eel shooting out from a crack in the coral, William's mothers hands shoot out and grab Tara by the upper arms and hold her fast. Tara gasps and shuts her eyes again.

William's mother whispers, "It's not me...it's..."

"William!", William booms, now standing taller and confident and grinning at Tara and his mother.

William's mother closes her eyes and winces. Tara opens her eyes wide to observe William who begins to elongate. William begins to eerily stretch from his middle upward and downward at the same time .His lithe and lean sixteen-year-old body becomes gaunt and skeletal and his skin yellows and cracks open. His soft fingers, that not so long ago brought pleasure, grow into formidable talons. His teeth protrude from his thin dry lips and his canines jut out six inches - glistening with digestive juices. William, now turns in the middle of the room, having morphed into a nine-foot monstrosity of muscle, stretched skin, teeth and tongue as it lolls out of his mouth and drips. William's mother and Tara stare back at him, transfixed.

William's eyes now glow, that same, demonic red and have an undeniable carnivorous intent. William, the creature, grins devilishly like a cat with a fluttering songbird clenched firmly in its jaws.

Mrs. Pudin stirs on the couch, sits up and rubs her eyes. When she can focus, the first thing she sees is William. Her measuring gaze begins at his feet and pans up much like a Japanese soldier confronted by Godzilla for the first time.

Testing the absorptive limits of her adult diaper, Mrs. Pudin squeaks, "Oh, dear! No more tea then?"

The End

SIKU

"Back again, Quilunaat?" asks Helen, an Inuit elder with leathery skin, who knows my name but prefers to call me ' white man '.

She wears a delightful mischievous smile and I just smile back and offer, "You too, kuluk?"

She laughs, "Better, but you still sound like an American tourist."

I feign hurt feelings and ask, "What are you after? Maybe I've seen it already?"

Helen ignores me, with a hand-wave dismissal, and continues to sort through the dump pile.

The dump pile is the focal point and social gathering place for anyone living permanently or temporarily in Aujuittuq. I came down today to look for an odd-sized cotter pin for my beat up snowmobile. It's not really mine. I inherited ' the beast ' from my predecessor and she didn't take care of it at all. I'll have to christen her when she is snow worthy. But that day seems far off.

How the hell does anyone get a job as a glaciologist and not know how to run and care for a snowmobile? I seethe just a little inside.

Guess I will never know as Melanie disappeared two months ago. They found all her stuff in her room, just as she left it. They found her snowmobile, now mine, and out of gas about ten kilometers out of Grise Fiord. It was as if she just got off and walked away. No body, no sign of a struggle or animal predator and no footprints – though to be fair they could have been covered over by the wind or the snow.

Helen catches me staring at the horizon as if in a trance, "Our tax dollars hard at work!"

"Hey, as soon as I find the part I need I'll be gone and then you'll be sorry and sad!" I joke.

"Remind me, what you're here for?"

"I'm a glaciologist. I study siku." I reply proudly hoping I haven't said anything inflammatory or disgusting by mistake.

Helen laughs, opens her arms wide and pivots three hundred and sixty degrees, "There isn't anything to study!"

She's right. The Inuit name for this hamlet means, ' the place that never thaws '.

The shoreline, usually covered in thick ice, is exposed and quite sandy and on a sunny day would look quite inviting. The local hunters can't navigate the free-flowing water, as it's too rough in its liquid state. A harsh existence is now even harsher if not impossible. It's not like you can buy a lot of groceries in the North. $ 6.99 for a wilting head of lettuce for example and why the hell do people buy lettuce anyway? It's devoid of any nutritional value!

I continue my hunt for the pin and I'm just about to call it quits when I spot a worn and dog-eared sketchbook. I dust it off and open it up. Not used as a sketch book but a journal and the owner had exquisite penmanship. I flip the pages hoping for something interesting. A few sketches of the tundra here and there and I note that the final entries are far from exquisite as they seem to be written by someone with a disturbed mind. I'm no psychologist or handwriting expert but the last entries are scrawled and all over the page as if the author might be losing it. The last date is the day that Melanie disappeared! I scan the inside front cover and sure enough, it's her journal!

How odd?

Why is it in the dump and why did I just happen to find it? And then there's the privacy question. Should I take it back to my room and read it? Wouldn't it be okay if she really is dead?

Did Anne Frank mind?

"What ya got there, Quilunaat?" asks Helen.

"Finders-keepers is the code of the junk pile!" I snap back.

Now why did I do that? Helen has been feisty but a worthy word-jouster.

She feigns hurt feelings then smiles, "Someone has a weasel up his butt! "

I smile, relieved that my only ' friend ' in the entire North is not offended.

"It's someone's journal," I offer.

"Any sexy stuff?" Helen asks quite seriously.

"I don't know." I reply, "I haven't had a chance to read it yet."

"Oh! Okay, well if you find any, let me know." she grins.

I laugh nervously, "Are you serious?"

She shrugs and grins and says, "You better seriously catch this!"

She throws something tiny in my direction and I instinctively snatch it out of the air and open my hand. It's the cotter pin I've been looking for and it looks like she even polished off the grime. I look up to thank her but she's already shuffling away from me and she waves goodbye without even looking back.

Back in my Spartan room and propped up on my bed, I begin to read Melanie's journal. It's hard to hold on to guilt when there's not much reading material in the North. It begins the day she arrived to start her assessment contract. The first third of the book is pretty hard going. It's all girl talk and it's like reading ' Twilight '. What the hell does a forty-year-old man (me) care about what goes on inside the head of a seventeen-year-old girl who wants to be a vampire! Thank God the movie didn't have a narration track!

Like, oh my God, like Edward's so cold like I wonder if it will like feel like a popsicle going in there when he like takes me like there!, I tee-hee-hee to myself.

But things start to get interesting the first time she gets out on the snowmobile. Okay! Speaking of which, I must come up with a name for ' the beast '. I haven't ridden her yet, as the weather has been too poor, but that cotter pin did the trick! I'll have

to buy Helen a head of lettuce in thanks! I can't call
' the beast ' Helen out of respect for Helen! And
Melanie seems a bit macabre since she may have
died on it! Hmmm now who starts to purr even
when t's cold?

    Bella!

    Sometimes, even I'm amazed at my incredible
wit and depravity. And this is one of those times!

    Bella it is!

Nov 04

Sleep hasn't come and I've been tossing and
turning for hours. You'd think I'd be able to sleep
now that we're through with the twenty-four hours
of sunlight but still no luck. I'm irritable and snap at
the slightest provocation.

Case in point, I met one of the locals at the dump.
Well I didn't actually meet her but she smiled and
whispered as she walked by me.

Kind of freaked me out and I turned on her and
yelled, "What the hell did you say ya leathery old
witch?"

She looks old and harmless – probably someone's
grandma! She didn't respond but kept on walking
and sounded like she was laughing. Make that
crazy grandma.

I went out on the sled for the first time today just
to see how she would run and get some practise in.
It's been years since I bombed around Lanark
County with my Dad and brothers. Felt pretty good
though and it's all coming back to me. The Ministry
really screwed me this contract, as it's bare bones.
The snowmobile they provided was probably

driven by Admiral Byrd in Antarctica. And now here it is in the Arctic still purring along.

I'm not sure if it's lack of sleep or what but some weird shit took place out on the tundra today. I could have sworn I heard whispering. Almost like someone was right behind me on the sled and whispering in my ear. I strained to make out the words but couldn't hear much over the noise of the engine. Whenever I stopped, the whispering would stop! Must be going a bit mental from sleep deprivation. Maybe just going mental.

I'll try and sleep.

Nov 16

Sleep has finally come but it's come with a price. I've been having the same dream, nightmare really, every night for days. I'm out on the tundra and a figure, all in shadow, beckons to me. He stands on a ridge and beckons to me with long and thin arms – too thin. The whole scene is bathed in an odd twilight kind of purple. He keeps whispering to me and even though he's far away, I can just make out the words.

"Dance with me, dance with us, dance upon the ice! The lights, the lights, summon the lights!"

I wake up in a cold sweat and can never get back to sleep. I've asked a few of the locals in a non-descript kind of furtive way - if they know anything? They are always polite but if they know anything, they seem reluctant to say. I met that elder I screamed at the other day.

I was walking on the beach when we passed one another; she smiled that mischievous smile and whispered, "The lights, the lights!!"

Nov 23

Losing my shit!
Messed up North.
Out on the sled every day this week.
Found the ridge from dreams.
Stopped sled warm up with some tea
Quiet. Nice
Looked up he was there – the spectre the ghoul.
Keep heading out later and later.
I want to be caught? Far way from Grise Fiord in
the dark!
Stupid risk!
Just stupit!
Concentrate you idoit!
He becks to me just like in the dream.
This time more than just one whisper.
Another language?
"The lights, the lghts!".
Messed up1
Start the sled and look back up.
There's two black shadowy spectres standing on
the ridge beckonin to me. I hightail it out of there
and make it back to the fiord.
No elation.
Sense of dread.
Go inside to get shitfaced and try and forget.
Up in the sky it's magic.
Northern Lights purple undulating and dancing.
They're waving to me!

    I see Helen, obviously returning from the dump,
manhandling an ATV tire. I rush over to her to see if
I can help.
    "Back off, Quilunaat!" she warns with her
mischievous grin, "I don't need your help!"

I laugh and surrender, "Okay. What are you going to do with that?" I ask starved for any information that might be new as it's in short supply in this hamlet.

"Gonna plant a rose garden." she smirks, "A rose would look good between your teeth as you prance along looking for the ice!"

"You get a rose to grow up here and I'll wear it!" I assure her

She lets the tire fall to the frozen ground and looks me over, "You're not so bad, Quilunaat! Perhaps you'll make it out of here alive after all."

I'm a bit gobsmacked at her comment but quickly recover and smile like I didn't notice.

I decide to go on the offensive, "Did you ever meet Melanie, the woman who was here before me, also looking for the ice?"

"Naw." she replies.

"Never whispered to her or said hello?" I press.

"Naw, just another Quilunaat!" Helen says, "Enough with the chatting, you're like an old woman!"

Helen gets the ATV tire moving again and doesn't give me another thought or word.

The weather keeps me fiord bound for a few days so I curl up and dive into Melanie's journal.

Dec 03
Don't feel like eating. drinking masturbate anymore
Don't call fiace fiancé who cares!
Ugly bastards!
so gaunt and filthy and emaciated.
black frostbite missing fingers and limbs.
What do they want?

Join them? show me? something they need?
whispering kaos white noise popping clicking
I never get any closer they never come to
bound to the ridge somehow
Where lies sleep?

I really don't know what to make of Melanie's journal? Sounds like the ravings of a lunatic and the government doesn't screen for nuttiness just the ability to work in isolation for long periods.

"Melanie, how would you describe your suitability for this position, aside from your credentials in glaciology?" asks the Government HR person.

"Well, I really enjoy long sessions of binge drinking, yelling at Inuit Elders, masturbating and creating hallucinations that whisper to me." Melanie proudly responds.

Do I feel sorry for her? No, not really. I'm leaning toward not giving a flying fuck. Crass I know but I'm beginning to see how this place got under Melanie's skin. I really have to stay focused and keep my anger under control as even the smallest things are setting me close to the edge. Of course the weather is not helping. It's been a white out for days and I'm itching to ride Bella! Who knows how far I'll have to drive just to find some ice? Probably more ice in one of Melanie's drinks! More white out means more Melanie.

Dec 06
Stupid! Stupit! Stipid!
storm blew in meter of snow.
ghouls on ridge hundreds lost count

beckon to me whisper then I catch some English.
"The ice,The ice. "
Dec 07
The ice. What FUCKING ICE!
Dec 13
No booze!
Don't remember a thing.
the smile! That shit eating grin from te same
woman!
spiton her mukluks
go somewhere civilized.
find some ice f eds progressreports.
no progress!
Dec 14
no voices
Dec 14 later that night
On way out drove past Elder,
"the ice, the ice"
laughed
ridge again.
Losing time in the dark.
Must have fallen asleep.
the voices "the ice, the ice."
ghouls reaching down to me.
help me?
grab ne? bony talons into my flesh wrench me over
ridge
limbs numb cold full dark.
gunned it back Fiord. purple Lights were dancing
and weaving between the ghouls dancing.

Finally a break in the weather! Gobbled down
some breakfast, then packed up Bella, and headed
out onto the tundra. What a great feeling – getting

out of Grise Fiord. Sometimes it's suffocating with the same faces day in and day out and nothing much to do. I decided to see if I could find the ridge that Melanie was so obsessed about. Maybe I'll find a clue to her disappearance and maybe I'll find the ice? Every living thing in this remote and harsh land depends on the ice. No wonder all the predators are emaciated including the ghouls! Hmm, is that how I see them now – ghouls? Getting to be as nutty as Melanie.

Dec 16
Spending all my time at the ridge
– I think?
beast's gas tank was empty.
I thought I had stayed in.
my reflexion. Jesus, lost a lot of weight.
"Come and see the ice, the ice, the ice"
Was I up on the ridge?
should gas up and head out there right now?
not ghouls
angels?
kinda weak
Lie down
Just a little while.

"Quilunaat! Time to go home. There's no ice here for you." Helen smiles at me with a sternness in her eyes.

Some of the other locals within earshot nod in agreement. The dump is busy today.

"You can't get rid of me so fast." I joke, "The feds want me to stay and complete my contract."

Helen uncharacteristically spits, "A contract one of our Inuit scientists could have won. But here you are Quilunaat! A fish out of water with no ties to the North."

"You can't be serious, playing the First Nations card!" I say incredulously, "I've done nothing to be disrespectful and I'm here because I care about you and your people and the environment. You think I like freezing my ass off in this one-sled town and being shunned by everyone I try and get to know?"

"Why should we know you? We didn't ask for your help. We know where the siku is because this is our land." Helen opens her arms to illustrate.

I stand there agog, not really believing that I'm publically being shunned by this Inuit elder who I thought I had an amicable connection with.

GAWD! I scream in my own head.

Words of rebuttal and regret are surging into my mouth but I have the presence of mind to stifle them and swallow them down. I hate this place right now! At this moment I wish I was back in Tofino riding the waves and warming up by the cedar beach fire. Maybe I should just catch the next flight out and leave Nunavut to Helen and her lot? I'm not welcome here or no longer welcome here and I can't find any ice to study. Not much of a life.

I turn to walk away from the dump and Helen and Aujuittuq and I wipe it all away with a hand gesture and mumble, "To hell with you!"

Dec 24
Dream? Nightmare? Crazy dream.
On the ridge. -----------Dancing on the ridge.
men, white men dancing on the ridge.

All shapes sizes.
funny old fashioned clothes.
fun!
dance and dance and dance.
The ridge, up in the sky.
We're dancing over the ice, ha ha dancing over rhe
ice and when o
ur clothes swish and way
– the static sound.
remember the ice, where the ice is.
everywhere.
Feel so good, so free.
Dancing over he ice in the purple lgt!.
Just want to keep dancing.
Don't wake up. Just dancing.
Siku, siku, siku everywhere!

Melanie's last entry. Did she really find the ice?
Bastards won't let me out of my contract or I forfeit
all the doe. I've decided I'll just ride Bella whenever
the weather holds and keep looking for the Ice. No
one in Grise Fiord gives a shit and I don't even get
that ' odd ' smile from Helen anymore. Last venture
out on Bella, I think I found Melanie's ridge. Pretty
damn high but I might try and climb up next time
I'm out. Who knows maybe there's ice on the other
side? Sure is quiet and peaceful out on the tundra.
Maybe that's why I'm here.

Perhaps the quietest place on earth and no
sounds of civilization at all. Could have sworn I
heard whispering out near the ridge but t was
probably just the snow blowing.

"Siku, siku, siku" the wind whispered.

Ha ha I'm in good company with Melanie. Nutbar! I think the locals are trying to put the scare in me. When I glanced up, to the top of the ridge, I just caught a glimpse of a dark thin figure beckoning to me. I'll bet it was Helen's idea, ungrateful cow!

"The ice, the ice, the ice..."

The End

THE TOLLING

Janine scans the interior of the Receiver Coffee shop as she hurries in from the cool and damp September air. She drags the toque off her freshly shaven head, loosens her scarf and unbuttons her black wool coat. The wonderful earthy smells of the café waft under her nose and her mouth waters. She gave up drinking the stuff months ago. Who knew guzzling down ten cups a day would give you the shits! Her eyes wander up to the glass sided balcony, the premo writing spot in all of Charlottetown! She spots her mother, Gracy, bent over her cell phone, clucking and laughing. She notices that her mom already has a latte so she looks through the tea list and disappointedly orders an Irish Breakfast.

Janine reorganizes all her cold weather clothes and plops down in front of her mom, still absorbed in her phone. Gracy is an older version of Janine except she has shoulder length curly salt and pepper hair, a plump body and a wonderfully wrinkled face.

"Like you're worse than like a teenager, like! " Janine teases.

Her mother holds up one hand and absently says, "Keep your knickers on!" then adds, "If you're wearing any?"

Janine laughs, "Cheeky old bat." which makes her mom smile.

"What's BBC?" her mother asks without looking up.

"British Broadcasting Corporation?" Janine offers.

Gracy frowns, "No, that can't be it. Flo says her son, Tom, is only interested in BBC!"

Janine spits out a mouthful of Irish Breakfast, sputtering, choking and laughing all at once.

Gracy finally looks up quizzically, "Something caught in your throat, dear?"

Janine doubles over in side splitting laughter, "ya a BBC!"

Then she completely looses it, banging on the table, and her mother joins in with more civilized titters and giggles.

When they come to their senses - under the watchful eye of fellow coffee shop goers - who tut tut at the very idea of having fun when there are blogs to be written and important memes to be sent.

Gracy motions to Janine's, barely touched Irish Breakfast, "How's your tea?"

Janine sighs, "My desiccated shit would taste better! They might know their coffee but their tea selection sucks."

"Next time we'll go to 4Good." Gracy suggests.

Janine snorts, "No, their Lapsang's too old – lost its punch!"

"But they have some nice fruity teas and roiboos." Gracy remembers.

"What the hell is the point! Fruit and tea and fruit in beer is a crime against humanity and what's the point of drinking red bush anyway?" Janine rages then calms herself. `

Gracy smiles re-assumingly.

"So what's Dad up to?" Janine asks.

Gracy ponders her question, takes a loving sip of her latte and replies, "Oh, he's off to the last crossing of the MV Holiday Atoll."

Janine tilts her head questioningly, "What for? It's just the final crossing of the season."

Gracy says excitedly, "No, it' s her final crossing ever, she's being retired."

Janine non- commitally says, "Oh."

Gracy gets more animated and starts using her hands to support her words, "Very exciting and your father is a VIP! I'm so glad they made a fuss about all those years he captained. I was worried he was becoming one of those older men who watch Y and R in the afternoon and discuss its merits with their other old male friends at Tim's. But the invitation put a spring in his step and stiffened his performance in the boudoir!"

Janine covers her mouth to laugh and roll her eyes.

"I made the crossing last month and everything seemed fine with the old girl!" Janine reveals.

"Well looks are deceiving, my dear. Apparently..." Gracy leans closer conspiratorially, "there's major structural deterioration and your father just about has a conniption every time she left the Wood Island terminal. He says she's an accident waiting to happen but the Feds won't spend a dime for upgrades."

"Holy shit!" from Janine.

"Holy shit, indeed!" from her mom.

Father Shay McGiven, tall, thin, full head of wavy black hair and an Irish accent so thick it makes Guinness seem watery, leans against a thick stone wall directly across from the bell tower door. Local fisherman/ casual contractor Alister Finch is barricading said door with orange cones and police tape.

"Is dat really necessary?" the Father asks.

Alister, a squat, thick sixty-year-old man with sandpapery skin, continues with his task.

"Course it is. Ya don't want anyone getting sick do ya?"

The Father looks concerned, "What ya mean sick? What's goin on in dair?"

Alister finishes with the barricade and stands up as tall as he can to face the priest. Which is quite impressive considering his four-foot-eight frame and three hundred pound bulk.

"It's bats, Father!" Alister pronounces with some seriousness.

The Father looks at him incredulously, "Bats? Wha?"

A grin creeps over Alister's face, "Right Father, you've got bats in yer belfry!"

The Father finally catches on and chuckles along with Alister, "You're a right bastard, making fun of a man of God!"

Alister pulls out a tightly rolled joint, lights it and takes a long drag.

He then holds it out to the priest, "Want a toot?"

The Father looks around, making sure the coast is clear, and helps himself, "Praise the Lord."

"Don't let anyone in there Father. The metal staircase is pulling out of the wall. I think it may come tumbling down." Alister offers.

"Shite!" spits the Father, "Where da hell are we goin ta find da money for dat? A bake sale?"

The two men laugh.

Father McGiven blows a well-practiced smoke ring to the heavens, "The Lord works in mysterious ways!"

The two men stare up and study the weather worn bell tower.

On board the MV Holiday Atoll, a full-blown gala is in full swing! The big sendoff for the original flagship is a study in opposites. The Holiday Atoll is old, battle -worn and creaking like an old woman's gnarled joints. She's really a floating rust bucket and well past her prime. The partygoers, mostly young and on the ' it ' list, dressed to the nines and sucking back the champagne like newborn piglets sucking the teats of their massive mother. A live jazz band plays ' Masquerade ' and as the afternoon has progressed they've turned up the PA to compete with the squealing piglets. As a result, no one hears the odd metallic straining, bumping and clanging.

Well almost no one.

The unusual noises haven't escaped Lyle's trained ears as former captain of the Holiday Atoll for over twenty-five years. Lyle is husband to Gracy and father to Janine and proudly wears a freshly pressed and starched Captain's uniform. The uniform is only honorary and only for this - the last day of service. Lyle is just about to venture below decks to suss out the strange noises when that loudmouth CEO stops him. He grabs Lyle's arm and leads him to the small podium in front of the band - playing that God awful jazz - which Lyle despises. The CEO, wearing a suit that probably cost as much as the CAT Ferry taps the side of his champagne glass trying to get the piglets attention. They're in full feeding frenzy gobbling down canapés and champagne so fast the waiters never make it to the other side of the room. This enrages the piglets that are only pleasantly pissed instead of full-blown wasted.

(A mutiny may be brewing!)

Finally the CEO glares at the band and makes the cut motion with his hand. Begrudgingly, the band cuts their jaunty rendition of ' Birdland ' short.

(Lyle is pleased to say the least.)

"Ladies and Gentleman, honored guests and a few dishonorable ones!" jokes the CEO.

A few drunken titters and moans but not the raucous belly laughs the CEO was hoping for.

Lyle doesn't even hear the words as he focuses his sonar-like hearing on the eerie sounds in the bowels of his beloved ferry. He'd run down to check it out if that jerkoff hadn't grabbed his arm again and was holding him fast. Lyle realizes he's missed most of the CEO's speech as all of a sudden he's propelled onto the podium to a very warm welcoming and heartfelt applause.

"So, is Dad getting a gold watch or anchor or something?" Janine asks slightly salivating at the sight and smell of her mother's latte.

Gracy makes a show of sipping her coffee and making her eyes roll up in mock pleasure.

"A medal maybe or a certificate! If those bastards won't fix the ferry they'll hardly splash out any doe on Lyle." Gracy sneers.

"It's nice that at least they're recognizing all those years of service and accident free at that! Can't have been easy sailing in the shite weather that's blown bigger vessels onto the rocks." Janine adds proudly.

Gracy beams at the unexpected praise from her daughter, who just usually rolls her eyes at everything her father says.

"I just hope he takes it easy with all the free flowing booze! You know how these things can get especially in the middle of the afternoon." Gracy stares into space in memory.

"Oh come on, Mom, it only happens once in a lifetime, so I hope he gets right legless!" Janine laughs.

Her mother turns scarlet but laughs too.

"He gets quite frisky when he's had a few!" Gracy confides.

Mother and daughter laugh together, not caring that the laptop crowd has been giving them the stink eye for the past thirty minutes.

Father McGiven, smiles to himself, as he reads a passage of Neil Gaiman's ' American Gods ' that he has hidden inside a rather large copy of the Bible. If someone unexpectedly walks in, it will look like the priest is thoroughly involved in his scriptures. But to the discerning eye, his glass of single-malt whiskey and the smile on his face are a dead giveaway. After all, who smiles when they read the bible?

(Satan maybe.)

And as fate would have it, his secretary, Donna, waltzes in unannounced and exclaims, "What are you doing here, Father?"

Father McGiven looks up in surprise, "Wha?"

"According to your schedule, you were supposed to bless the final crossing of the Holiday Atoll and right now!" Donna says a bit too dramatically.

The Father's jaw drops.

"Oh, shite!" is all he has to offer in response.

"Too late?" he asks.

"Too late." Donna confirms.

Lyle leans up against the bar and glances down at all the drinks lined-up in his honor. He grins broadly, remembering the standing ovation he received after his speech. He tries to count all the well wishers who shook his hand and contributed to the line of drinks. He didn't think he would, but he sure likes the feeling of being the center of attention. He's in such a fine mood that even that jazz music is starting to make sense and he taps his foot in time.

Probably not 4/4. he thinks and laughs at his own wit.

He knows he's way over his booze limit just because he's usually not that funny. An observation echoed frequently by his daughter, Janine, who takes great satisfaction in tormenting him whenever she comes for a visit. Man, they get on each other's nerves! He loves her and he knows the feeling is mutual. The band takes a break and the piglets hoof it forward to replenish their drinks from the free bar - which Lyle is currently holding up.

Good time to bleed the iguana he thinks to himself, laughs to himself and unsteadily makes his way to the head.

As soon as he leaves the party, his own head clears a bit and the hum of the engines replaces the din of the festivities. Lyle passes a roped off open hatch, that leads to the ' crew only ' lower decks, where the engine and other essential goodies are housed. Two loud BANGS followed by what sounds like two ricochets draws Lyle's attention to the bottom of the darkened hatchway. He scans three hundred and sixty degrees and makes sure the coast is clear. He knows he's a VIP today and no longer Captain and shouldn't stick his nose into the crews business. He should just report it and go take a piss like he planned. But screw it! Buoyed by the numerous drinks he has drunk in his own honor,

Lyle unhooks the rope and descends the metal stairs into the ships nether regions.

Janine ebbs and flows her way back to the table with two raspberry scones, on a plate, and sets them down on the table.

Gracy admires the pastry and says, "Those look good! Thanks dear,"

Janine sinks down, looking a bit distracted.

"See a ghost?" her mother inquires.

Janine spits, "Worse! My ex."

Gracy scans the room trying to fix eyes on Shane, Janine's ex sports lots of cool tattoos but not many brains as Gracy recalls. His life goals consisting of screwing Janine and writing scripts on something called ' FinalDraft '. He hasn't sold a thing in five years and thankfully Janine saw the light and banished him from her room and her womb.

"Better off without him!" Gracy consoles.

"Ya, think?" Janine grimaces.

All of a sudden, the entire café reverberates with the sound of what must be a monstrous bell!

 BONG!

Janine, and her mother, hold on to the edges of their table as smaller items such as cups and teapots and plates vibrate onto the floor with a crash. Some of the regulars shriek as the screens on their precious laptops shatter in spider-web patterns.

A few of the café's main panes of glass begin to crack. The sound of untold numbers, of those ridiculous car alarms, fill the air.

When the vibrations stop, Janine and Gracy look at one another in terror and at the same time say, "What the hell was that?"

Donna, Alister and Father McGiven race outside and meet up at the base of the bell tower. Alister grips one of the boards he screwed over the door and gives it a tug but it holds fast just the way he left it.

"No one's been through that door, Father!" Alister states confidently.

"Den what the feck is goin on?" The Father says out loud but meant to say in his inside voice.

"These are the only working bells in town, where can it have come from?" Donna hopes for an answer.

"Sure no one else was in dar when you boarded er up?" the Father asks already knowing the answer.

"If you're thinking someone got trapped in there and rang the bell for help, you're grasping at straws." Alister warns.

"Could it be the ascension?" Donna, the most pious of the lot, asks.

"Get real!" the Father sneers, "more likely the Sidhe, those tricksy bastards!"

Donna looks crestfallen and Alister grins at the remark.

Out of the corner of his eye, Lyle sees a bullet-like object shoot out of the metal wall and he ducks just in time.

GONG!

The object, a rusted rivet, imbeds itself in the facing wall with a metallic clang.

"That was close," Lyle sighs,

He creeps over to the wall from which the rivet was shot. He maneuvers as low as possible to avoid unnecessary holes in his head and death. Still crouching, he examines the boiler wall that flakes off at his touch. Some of the rivets have blown off just like the one Lyle witnessed.

This is not good!

Upon further inspection, he notices steam escaping from the boiler where no steam should be. The metal has begun to bulge and turn color to reflect the intense heat building-up inside. He's also noticed the heavy stench of diesel fuel and exhaust and his mouth begins to water. Too much alcohol and the fumes take their toll on poor Lyle, the VIP, the retiree and he doubles over. Lyle fights back the burning bile which demands its freedom.

Another rivet is spit from the boiler sounding like a church-bell's bong.

Bong!

The position of the MV Holiday Atoll and the currents it crosses turn the bong into a deafening reverberating ...

BONG!

The rivet deflects off the facing metal wall and falls to the hull. But on its way down, it lands on Lyle's calf as the noise and the nausea have forced him to his knees. He SCREAMS out in pain as the red-hot rivet burns through his skin and doesn't stop until it hits bone. Lyle tries to pry it out with his fingers but it's buried in his flesh. The rivet blisters the tips of his fingers and sizzles the muscle and fascia of his calf.

I have to get out of here! Lyle says in his inside voice.

He pulls himself along the greasy hull, toward the rusty metal ladder that leads to the upper decks.

I've got to warn them! he convinces himself as his hand slips on the oil and grease and he takes a header to the decking which opens him up just over his right eye.

The café is in chaos! The, normally sedentary, hipsters clamber over, beat-back and push over their fellow café office colleagues in an attempt to be the first one to either:

A] Post pictures of the debris to social media

B] Head to the brewpub to compare their social media pictures of the debris

C] Run away as fast as their un-socked feet can take them

Janine, although not surprised, is still dismayed at their anti-social behavior as she helps her mother Gracy navigate the littered staircase down to the main floor. Just as they exit the building to join others who are milling about on the street, another massive BONG sounds.

BONG!

Everyone holds their hands over their ears - trying to lesson the effects of the sound and a few people fall to the pavement, momentarily struck with vertigo.

Janine manages to keep Gracy upright and pull her out of the way of a police cruiser that rockets past - lights flashing and sirens blaring.

"JESUS!" Janine shouts at the car, already far down the street and beyond hearing range.

"You okay mom?" she asks.

Gracy cocks her head at Janine and says, "What?"

Father McGiven is helped to his feet by Alister and Donna and they all stand unsteadily, in a loose circle, trying to steady themselves.

Alister offers, "Its not our bells Father! Seems to be coming off the water."

"Such an unearthly sound? Like da hell mouth opening!" The Father exclaims.

Donna crosses herself, even though she's Presbyterian, just for good measure.

Father McGiven scratches his head, "Ya don't suppose dis has anything ta do wit the Holiday Atoll?"

Alister shrugs and Donna pulls out a rosary, no one knew she had, and goes to it like the Pope himself.

Lyle looks blearily up at the ceiling. Not at all surprising as the blood from his cut drips into both eyes. He rolls over and dry-heaves. He grits his teeth and steadies himself on the same oily railing that let him down before. This time he's aware of its greasy condition. Slowly but surely, he makes slow steady progress up the stairs - spitting frequently as the rising bile causes him to salivate. Above decks, the fresh air hits his sweaty and bloody face and he staggers over to the railing to hurl over the side. At that very moment, the last rusted-out rivets - tasked with the task of keeping the ferry held together – fail!

Three rivets, this time, sail into the opposing wall and bury themselves in the metal causing a thunderous BONG! BONG! BONG! The pressure released, the ferry tips violently to the ley side. The same side Lyle has decided to spew his guts out!

The ferry lurches and Lyle is propelled into the ocean like an acrobat from a circus cannon.

The glass, from all the cars parked and moving on Richmond Street, explodes into a million tiny shards rocketing into passengers and pedestrians and anything else in it's path. The shards embed into soft surfaces like flesh and hard surfaces like concrete in equal measure. Sheets of glass fall, from shop windows, onto the sidewalks. It falls on anything that happens to be on those sidewalks like men, women, children and dogs who are killed and maimed by the guillotine motion, as it crashes to the earth. Their screams go unheard as everyone nearby experiences a temporary high-pitched tone in their ears. Said organs try and deal with the giant bell-like sounds emanating from the ocean and reverberating off the buildings into the streets.

Bleeding, but more or less unscathed, Janine and Gracy wriggle out from the underside of an abandoned delivery van. They stand on shaking limbs and wordlessly make sure they are both okay and shake the glass out from their clothes.

They study their surroundings which resembles a battlefield. They think that this is what it must have looked and felt like in the blitz, being bombarded by the Germans or even worse being fire bombed by the Canadians in Dresden! Both woman shiver and look at one another with pleading eyes.

Gracy mouths the words, "Lyle!"

Janine mouths, "The ferry terminal!"

They both nod then set off on foot, knowing there is no other way to get there.

Father McGiven and Alister crouch over Donna, who sits limply, and unconscious, her back against the bell tower wall. She's been struck with falling debris from the tower and her normal crisp church-lady appearance is now a disheveled mess of dust, crumbling rock and dried blood.

Alister pats the Father on the arm and with the other continues to monitor Donna's faint pulse, "She's alive! Barely so but alive all the same."

The Father gently removes the rosary from her clenched fist.

"Fat lot o good dat did!" Father McGiven says and then tosses the rosary, uncaringly, to the side.

Their attention is drawn to the boarded up door, of the bell tower, not by a sound or anything tangible but by a feeling.

A feeling of despair and panic.

Standing in front of the door - is the CEO. He's dripping wet and shivering and is trying to communicate something to the two men. His mouth is moving very fast but no sound is coming out. Alister looks down, at the cobblestones, under the CEO which are dry as a bone.

"Whatch ya saying man, we can't understand you?" the Father pleads, "Whatcha doin ere anyway, miss the ferry?"

The CEO looks deeply into the Fathers eyes and holds him fast with an eerie stare, then shakes his head slowly from side to side. The CEO then turns and walks through the boarded up bell tower door - as if t were a mere projection.

Father McGiven and Alister take a step back and involuntary hold on to one another for support.

"What the fuck!" inhales Alister who immediately turns scarlet and blubbers an excited, "Sorry Father."

Father McGiven pays him no mind and strains his neck to study the belfry.

"JAYSUS?" exclaims the Father as Alister follows his gaze.

And high up in the belfry of the bell tower, the CEO pulls down hard on the bell rope.

Bong! Bong! Bong!

Anyone in Charlottetown, not deafened by the surging bells of the sea, turns to look at the church as the bells ring at a time that they usually don't. Can't be a service as it's mid afternoon and didn't that Father McGiven say they were needing money for bell tower repairs? This day and all it's happenings is certainly out of the ordinary and the good folk of PEI do not like out of the ordinary!

(Move to Toronto or Montreal if you're looking for oddballs and such things and while you're there tell the big mucky-mucks at the CBC to knock it off with Anne of Green Gables! She's been resurrected

*three times already and we don't need a fourth so
move on to another story for God's sake!)*
Bong! Bong! Bong!
*Has anyone been counting? Seems like it's never
going to stop!*

Lyle smacks into the ocean like a chubby nine-
year-old at a public pool birthday party whose just
been double-dog-dared to dive off the high
platform of the deep end. Any effect, his way more
than usual drinking spree had caused, was quickly
washed away when the icy brine washed over him
and momentarily pulled him under. He sputters
and coughs his way to the surface and treads
water. It takes a few seconds to get his bearings
but when he catches sight of the MV Holiday Atoll,
listing and taking on water, he swims like a man
possessed away from the ferry. *(Sailors being
sucked into the wake of a sinking ship is no myth).*
Lyle's goal is to die of a quick heart attack watching
Arsenal win the Champions League rather than
being diced and sliced by the ships propeller.

Two ancient Coast Guard helicopters thunder
overhead in the direction of the Woodland
Terminal where Janine and Gracy have just arrived.
They are foot-worn and resemble Syrian refugees
emerging from yet another American airstrike. And
the description is apt. The volunteers, who have set
up a first aid triage station, are mostly from Syria
and they grimace and reminisce about the joy of
being taken in by this country and the loss of their
original homeland. The two women, Gracy and
Janine, are escorted to a line of similarly disheveled

PEI- ers who one by one get checked over by a field doctor. The closest Tim's must have gotten wind of the emergency as take-out cups of coffee are thrust into Janine's and Gracy's hand. Gracy is about to explain that her daughter doesn't drink coffee but before she can - Janine has practically drained her cup and is searching for more.

The first helicopter, to land at the makeshift LZ, is laden with heavy body bags. As the bags are extricated and unzipped it becomes obvious that - no one minded the rough ride, as they are all quite dead. Their fancy dress clothes still dripping and drenched and their faces already starting to look gaunt and drained and a little bloated.

Janine, fueled by caffeine, is the first runner to make it to the assembled corpses and she flies from one to the next looking for her dad.

She straightens up, waves to her mom and even smiles when she yells, "He's not here!".

Gracy raises a fist to the sky, like she's just scored the decisive Arsenal Champions League winning goal and thanks the Gods that her Lyle may still be alive!

Alister and the Father turn when they hear Donna cough and realize that they are no longer alone. Craning their slightly bloated and purple-tinged necks to stare up at the belfry are two men and a woman. Their heavy wet clothes droop on their bodies and their hair is plastered to the sides and front of their faces. They appear to be unaware or uncaring of their surroundings and just fix their gaze on the bell-ringing specter of the CEO, who tolls the bell two more times.

Bong! Bong!

As the Father and Alister attend to the recovering Donna, a soaking wet man and woman join their comrades around the bell tower and begin their vigil.

Lyle, sleepily, treads water as he watches the helicopters hoist the bodies from the sea. His beloved Holiday Atoll takes one final bow, in her death throes, and then sinks under the frothing water with swift dignity.

I really should start swimming towards the helicopters, he thinks.

But thinking is requiring a great deal of effort as the gentle hands of hypothermia begin to rock him.

"Just a little nap and then I'll be rested." he mumbles to himself.

Bong! Bong! Bong! Bong! Bong! – faintly in the distance.

What an odd dream. Me going to church! Lyle laughs to himself and gets a mouthful of sea water which he quickly spits out, annoyed.

Bong! Bong! BONG! BONG! BONG!

"BLOODY BELLS!" he screams now fully awake.

Lyle tries to shake himself into even more wakefulness but soon realizes that his muscles have cramped and seized up from the exchange of heat and cold.

"Got to swim! Got to swim to the wreckage where they can see me! Damn it arms WAKE THE HELL UP!" Lyle frantically calls out.

He begins to thrash about realizing that death by Champions League is ebbing away like his life.

"HEY! OVER HERE!" A few voices ring out.

Lyle stops thrashing and treads water to gain his bearings and the bearings of the voices. To his right, at about one hundred meters, he sees a small group of people and some of them are waving to him. He waves back to acknowledge he's seen them and begins to stiffly swim in their direction. Hope and self-preservation begin to course through his veins and the feeling gradually comes back to his shivering limbs.

The perimeter of the bell tower has become crowded. More and more witnesses join the throng of phantoms who gawk up at the CEO. His bell ringing doesn't seem to be slowing down.

Father McGiven has given up trying to communicate with the sodden assemblage and sits, on the cobblestones, and marvels at the sight. Alister has taken Donna inside to administer first aid and so he won't have to explain - why a ring of ghouls, now three-deep, have decided to haunt the grounds. To be quite honest, Alister is just happy to be as far way as possible as they give him the heebie-geebies!

Only a few meters left and Lyle can see that the people, men and woman, have locked arms in a small huddle and they all wear sailors uniforms.

They all smile when they recognize Lyle and the First Mate says, "Glad to see you made it Captain!"

Lyle smiles back at the respectful compliment, "How many survivors?"

Their smiles turn south as they avoid Lyle's hope filled face.

"This is it Sir!" the First Mate reports quietly.

The huddle opens up, so Lyle can lock his arms in, and they close the circle once more to stay warm and conserve energy. No one says a word as the gravity of an already grave situation is mulled over in each mind.

Lyle breaks the silence, "When she first listed, I was thrown clear."

The others nod, still in mulling mode. The First Mate chimes in, as do the others, and all their reports have odd similarities and the fact that they all survived unscathed, at least physically, seems miraculous!

The First Mate sighs, "Someone was looking after us."

Lyle adds, "It was the Holiday Atoll. Her last act was to look after those who had looked after her all these years. Three cheers for the old girl! Hip hip!"

"HOORAY!"

"Hip hip!"

"HOORAY!"

"Hip hip!"

"HOORAY!'

Father McGiven takes a sip of the whiskey that Alister brought him seemingly hours ago, "Seventy seven,"

Seventy-seven ' Bongs ' high up in the bell tower and then complete silence.

Not a birdcall, an insect wing or a dog barking could be heard. Even the helicopters, still working in the distance, flew silently.

The Father painfully rises, after sitting in the same spot for so long, and rubs his legs as he strains to catch a glimpse of the CEO in the fading light. And like the fading light, the CEO slowly fades out of existence as he looks toward the ocean and hangs his head. And all around the bell tower, the amast seventy-seven souls turn toward the sea and begin to fade as well with the veiled crimson sun as it sinks below the salty water.

The Father is left standing all alone, wondering what he has been a part of and how is it possible? And does it really matter anyway? He prays a team of scientists don't come in and try and explain it all away as a mass hallucination or mass reaction to some airborne pollutant.

Janine and Gracy huddle on the back of an ambulance wrapped in scratchy blankets. They sit, in stunned silence, with the news that the last helicopter is in bound and that almost all of the bodies have been recovered. The chopper may come back empty-handed. The women have made it through, the long day, by rushing to each helicopter as it came in - trying to find Lyle. So far they haven't seen him and they have all but given up hope. They've done their part - consoling those alive who have positively identified their own loved ones. But there's only so much energy one can give to another family when their own may have been torn apart.

The Press have squirmed their way in like maggots to a dead sheep, devouring everything in their path and giving nothing in return. Janine and Gracy have declined all attempts at interviews and

Janine's hand still aches from punching the nose of an invasive camerawoman. And now that the day is ending and the daylight fading, they have all picked out the best location to shoot the last helicopter returning from it's last run. They are very excited as it's the ' money shot ' and they, being the good maggots that they are, can smell the bonus money!

The last chopper flies in, in front of the descending bloody sun, as if it's a scene from Coppola's ' Apocalypse Now '. The only thing missing is the voice over and The Doors. The helicopter sets down heavily and a few camera lights blink on illuminating the sliding doors which creak open. The interior remains dark as the puny camera lights can only pick out a few shapes of unknown origin.

Janine and Gracy have pushed their way to the front of the gathered crowd. Rival news crews give them a wide birth after witnessing Janine's ferocity!

Bursting out of the helicopter door, and into the harsh light and camera flashes, jumps Lyle - wrapped in a shiny emergency blanket. He searches the faces, with one hand trying to block the unnatural camera light, and his eyes fall on Gracy, his beautiful Gracy, his best friend and love of his life. And right beside her, their daughter Janine who gets under his skin and whom he loves unconditionally. But instead of rushing toward them and jumping into their arms, he holds his ground and just drinks them in. Tears gush, from tired eyes, as the warmest smile breaks Lyle's tired face. A smile that melts the hearts of everyone assembled at the ferry dock and makeshift morgue.

Janine and Gracy bask in the sight of their beloved Lyle whom they thought was dead. Lyle stands tall before them, bathed - not in the glare of the camera light - but in the glow of their love for one another.

The End.

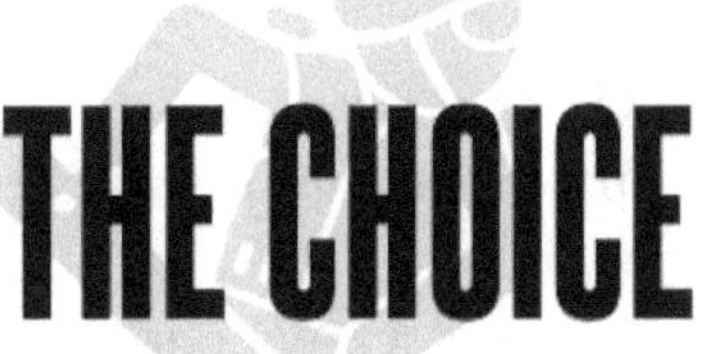

THE CHOICE

Floating.

Floating in deep, dark, blackness. It buoys me up like warm viscous oil, licking and sliding along my inert form. In the distance, a white pinprick that the blackness undulates towards, expanding and pulsing.

My eyes hurt.

My closed eyes hurt.

Agony!

It pumps like God-awful Top 40 music, throbbing in my temples and circulating in my blood stream.

Gawd!

Floaters zigzag across my vision and tears seep out my closed eyes. The pounding pain — excruciating!

Birds chirping?

A stream gurgling nearby?
Wet dog?
Meat?
I raise my head and reel in nauseous vertigo.
Bile burning my throat. I push up onto my forelegs
and begin to dry heave rhythmically.
Forelegs?
Gack! Gack! Gack! Gack!
My whole body spasms as I empty my guts.
Disgusting!
Steaming blood, hair and a few bones.
Cheese curd? Jesus, just how messed up did I
get last night?
Shaking like a newborn, I follow the burbling of
the stream through the woods and I drink and drink
and drink — trying to slake a bottomless thirst.
This water tastes cold and sweet. Delicious!
I snap my head up! My senses are amplified.
My sight, sense of smell and my hearing can be
focused now like a telescoping lens. If this is a side-
affect of blackout level debauchery, then bring it
on! I look down at the water.
What the hell?
From the shining surface of the stream, some
kind of animal looks back at me quizzically. I snort.
The animal snorts back then bares its formidable
teeth. Some kind of canine. My teeth feel dry and I
realize my mouth is open and I lick my teeth, close
my jaw and shake my head. Particles of a familiar
scent melt on the receptors of my nose. I sniff the
air and follow it and as it gets stronger, I realize
that I know it from a memory.
Two wolves trot toward me, fur bristling,
growling and slavering. They're massive, much

bigger than a grey wolf and perhaps two times their size and mass. I freeze, heart pumping. It's fight or flight and I stand my ground and taste the air.

Taste the air?

I know these wolves. They sniff the air, withdraw their canines and wag their tails. They know me.

Trevor? Greencard?

They sniff again, "Angus?"

In unison the three of us exclaim, "What the hell? You're a wolf!"

"NO, you're a wolf!"

"What?"

"How?"

"Trevor stop sniffing my ass!" I growl.

Trevor hunches his shoulders, "Sorry man, I can't help it! Wow, you drank a lot last night."

"I don't remember shit about last night," I whine.

Trevor continues, "And poutine, Tons of poutine!"

Slurp, lap, slurp, and slurp.

Trevor and I turn towards the sound. Greencard laps at his balls. He becomes self-conscious and stops.

"You know you always wanted to. It's awesome!"

Slurp, slurp, gobble, and slurp.

Splayed out and slobbering on his own lap is Trevor. He's washing his balls with his tongue and his pink penis is peeking out of it's sheath. My tail curls skyward and I growl fiercely at one then the other.

"Can we stop this ball licking orgy for one second and try to figure out what's happened to us?"

They keep licking!

I pounce on Trevor and clamp down on his throat, sinking my teeth in. He yelps and exposes his neck in submission. I shake him, a bit, for good measure then let him go. Greencard has stopped licking and he and Trevor get up on all fours and lower their heads, tails between their legs.

Holy shit! I'm the Alpha!

I growl and lunge at them, gnashing my teeth and they flinch and back away.

Ha, ha, I just might mount these assholes!

I take a breath, "Okay, does anyone remember what happened? How we got here? Where here is? And why did we morph into wolves?"

We all snap our heads to the West in unison.

"Oh my God! A SQUIREEL!"

With ancestral grace and power, we bound off after the terrified creature. I am filled with exquisite joy as I dig my claws in and leap over logs and slide through the bush. I growl deep in my chest to express and celebrate my aliveness – the most alive I have ever felt. We twist and turn, snapping at the squirrel and each other in encouragement. Deep down inside we know we will never catch the squirrel and even the squirrel knows it. The squirrel races up a tall tree, scolding us from the safe heights. We give up and lope back to the stream and noisily drink our fill. We lay on the bank, panting and sprawled out, happily exhausted.

I give my head a good shake, "That was terrific!"

Greencard nods and licks his lips, "I almost had him, you know, but I didn't want the chase to end too soon."

"Bullshit!"

"Oh my God, you have got to try this!"

Greencard and I turn our heads toward Trevor who's on his back squirming and writhing in delight.

Trevor sighs, "I don't know what it is or how long it's been dead but I'm going to cover myself in it!"

Greencard jumps to his feet, "Can I have a turn?"

Trevor spits, "No way Dude, find your own!"

My tail bristles and curls stiffly up into the air. I pounce on Greencard, dig my dewclaws into his ribs and start humping. I think about all the times he's cock-blocked me, borrowed money and got us kicked out of the pub.

In other words, I'm really pounding him.

Greencard yelps, "WHAT THE HELL, DUDE?'

Trevor laughs and I growl and grab Greencard's neck, "It's not like it's gay or anything!"

Greencard struggles to get free, "Get off you BASTARD, this isn't funny!"

"It's not supposed to be stupid! I'm claiming the Alpha role!"

He's had more than enough so I climb off and give my body a good shake.

Our ears pull back and we all sniff the air, alert to the pheromones of another different smelling wolf.

Trevor, "Who's that?"

Leaping silently out of the brush is a sleek black female. She stands solidly and regally in front of us and curls back her lip to reveal her beautiful yet lethal pearl white fangs.

I submit to her immediately, my tail curls under me and I avoid her fierce eyes.

Why did I do that? Body, why have you forsaken me? I scold myself.

She grins devilishly, "Bonjour, mais enfant. Aimez-vous les changements que j'ai faits?"

Greencard looks quizzically my way, "What? I haven't spoken French since grade nine."

Trevor, "Wait a sec, if she's speaking French then either we're in France or Quebec?"

Greencard, "Or New Orleans!"

Trevor, "That's N'Orlins, dumbass!"

I pipe in, "Well, it can't be France cuz it's so guttural."

She holds her head up majestically, "Snobs!"

Greencard takes a stab, "esque tu a Quebecois ou Creole?"

She replies slowly and as guttural as possible, "Que-be-cois!"

Collectively, we all spit, "Damn!"

The last time we were in Quebec, we got absolutely legless at the Impact game. We were wasted but behaving ourselves, for a change, and even declined an invitation to brawl in the stands. On the way to a pub after the game, we got jumped and had the crap kicked out of us. Then the Surette picked us up and kicked the remaining crap out of us and dumped us back in the same alley. Suffice it to say, that we have no fond memories of Quebec.

My turn to speak French, "ou est ah tou? Montreal? Quebec City?"

She shakes her head, "No, idiot, you're near St.Jerome."

Greencard moans, "The anus of the world in any language! How did we get here?"

She cocks here head, "You don't remember? The Laneway Festival? You guys asked me for x?"

Trevor, "Did we have fun?"

She laughs then howls, "You turned into wolves, didn't you?"

We all join the howling. This is so cool! It's a hive mind kind of thing and I am connected to all wolves and all the wolves there have ever been – all the way back to the first wolves. We stop and nip and bite each other excitedly, pumped on adrenaline.

I stare into her deep green eyes, "But we'll change back right?"

She cocks her head again, "Why would you want to do that? As wolves, we are free! No government. No taxes. We eat and sleep and fuck whenever we want. We don't kill one another and most of the time we just run around and play!"

Trevor, "Don't forget about rolling in the dead shit!"

Greencard, "Or the ball licking!"

"So what? You guys are all cool with this?" I inquire.

"Ya, pretty much. My old life is shit!" Greencard says matter of factly,

Trevor chimes in, "Ya me too. My girlfriend kicked me out and I'm in debt about three hundred grand."

"Wait a minute. Don't you own a condo? Isn't that the good kind of debt?" I pose.

Trevor laughs, "Aw, that's bullshit! It's a lifetime of debt with a nice bow tied around it!"

She nuzzles my muzzle, "And you baby? It's not just us. I run a pack and we are badass!"

"I don't know?" I quip. "This is all so sudden"

Greencard practically has his nose up her butt, sniffing for all he's worth.

Trevor is no better, flopping on his back in front of her and offering his throat in slutty submission.

"Are the legends true? Do we turn on the cycle of the full moon? Silver bullets?" I ponder.

"merde! Are you serious?" Shaking her head back and forth. "It's a lab mutation from a DNA therapy experiment that tried to edit DNA in the human body."

I rack my canine brain, "Military?'

"non, police."

"Police?"

She nods, "oui, they wanted to modify the Surette to become more aggressive."

"MORE AGGRESSIVE?" us Anglos quip.

"That explains a lot," I murmur to myself.

Trevor, "So, how the hell did we get it?"

She laughs, "I talked you into getting tattoos. I always use the same needle."

Greencard extracts his nose from her butt, "What the hell? A dirty needle! We could have aids for Gods sake!"

She reassures us, "You'll never be sick a day in your life! Just one of the perks of turning."

Trevor chides Greencard, "You turned into a wolf and you're worried about STD's?"

She bares her teeth and growls, "It's time to go. Decide one way or the other?"

Trevor, "In!"

Greencard, "In!"

Me, "Out!"

Trevor, "Out? You pussy! Why?"

Me, "It's been fun and all but I have a good life to go back to!"

Greencard, "Oh, so you're better than us, is that it?"

Me, "Damn straight!" I laugh, "I'm happy for you guys and for you - I think it's the right move. It's just not for me and I'm looking forward to turning back."

She stares sadly at me.

"I will turn back right?" I ask filled with hope.

She growls and snaps at me and leaps off into the bush, "C'mon you two!"

Greencard and Trevor bound after her like puppies trying to get the treat first.

I bark my goodbyes as they disappear, swallowed by the dark woods. Crazy canine delinquents! I wish them well. In this debt-ridden society, where else is there to go? Go bankrupt, like the majority of the country, or turn into a werewolf!

I don't remember much about the past three days. A half-memory of loping along looking for civilization, looking for help. **I raise my head and examine myself.**

I'm naked.
I'm filthy.
But I'm human by God, human!
I close my eyes and fall back, as if I'm falling into a cool pool on a scorching summer day. I revel in my humanness.
Scratchy. Scratchy, under my bare back?
I bolt upright.
Scratchy stinky blanket, fluorescent lights, steel toilet, steel sink, steel bars!
"A jail cell!"
The outer door creaks open like a medieval dungeon-door might.

Completely filling the doorframe is a huge man, resembling ' The Hulk ' but a little less green. He wears a Surette uniform and carries coffee and a croissant on a silver cafeteria tray. He lumbers over and thrusts the food through a rectangular hole in the bars with a giant fist. I clutch the offering in trembling hands and my stomach reminds me that I haven't eaten in days. The shaved gorilla, in the cop uniform, smiles down at me and studies my crotch. I'm terrified, my brain offering up gruesome possibilities about what this might mean.
Thanks brain, you jerk!
Its mouth begins to open. I'm expecting "ugh" or perhaps just a grunt.
But he shrugs and says, "Huh, I didn't notice that when they brought you in."
He smiles and looks at my face, "I'll make a call and you'll be outta here soon."
He lumbers out the door, cell shaking with each footfall, and closes the door with a slam.
Once again I'm alone.

So, what was he looking at?
I get excited!
Does becoming a werewolf mean a bigger dick?
I spread my legs and study my junk.
Hmm, looks to be the same length and girth.
Wait a minute, my pubes are shaved off and I know I didn't do that.
Is that a tattoo?
She wasn't lying!
It's a depiction of Romulus and Remus and their surrogate wolf mom.
Huh! Well that's sort of cool.
My eyes wander to my scrotum.
It looks good.
Better than I remember.
I mean not just aesthetically but my balls look like they taste good.
Now, if I can just reach down far enough ...

The End

THE LAKE

A tranquil, opaque, blue-tinged lake stretches out and shimmers in the oppressive summer heat - reminiscent of the Dead Sea. Through the haze, a thin elderly bird-like woman strides out of the watery depths like a great blue heron. She stilts along the shoreline, dressed in a robin's egg blue robe, occasionally stopping to peer into the shallow water at her bare feet.

Two adventuresome crows scold and swoop down on the woman, trying to make a name for themselves in the cooler corvidae circles.

The woman will have none of it and shoes them away with a heron-like "GROK ".

She glides onto the shore, on spindly legs, and strides away from the lake with a more human-like gait but still a bit stiff and unnatural.

Only a little way down the dusty dirt road, a thirty-something couple amicably terminate their relationship. They share a small circular beer stained table on the upper level of a rundown bar called ' The Ukrainian Hall '. Not the most inventive name, mind you, but they do serve a mean cabbage roll and the beer is cold and tastes the same as any Canadian beer in any bar in Canada.

(Beer which could be described, with much affection, as horse piss!

It gets the job done and still gets the American tourists shitfaced as their beer equivalent might be described as weak horse piss from a horse that had a urinary tract infection or had in fact been dead for several months.)

But that was far from the minds of said couple. He is tall and lanky with a long scraggly unkept beard and no socks in leather loafers *(filthy hipster!)* and she with her unkept kinky locks pushed down under a John Deere baseball cap.

(Would it be a stretch of the imagination to think that she had never seen a tractor or played baseball and that he not only owned socks and a razor- ordered online from Henry - no doubt!)

The old woman slinks into the same bar. Her sharp bird-like eyes fall on the couple as if on a succulent grub feasting on a bloated water plant. She studies them with anticipation. When the couple laughs, stands and hugs one another goodbye, she looks crestfallen. The couple or ex-couple sweep past her, she tastes the air and snorts in dismay. The old woman scans the room, almost empty except for the usual bar flies mumbling to themselves and occasionally wolfing down a pickled egg. She sighs in resignation and is about to turn around and go back to the lake when a young crying woman bolts past her and out of the bar. The girl's tears hang and linger in the air and the old woman sticks out her tongue and savors their salty tang.

She smiles, then slips out the door in pursuit of the young woman. No one notices her departure. Not the barkeep or the regulars or the hand drawn sign by the front door which exclaims that bowhunks will be denied service!

Outside, the sun makes it's low descent as the shadows rise and gain strength.

The crying woman, bathed in crimson hues, shakes and releases her grief unabated by the etiquette of societal norms. She is quite young with long flowing blond hair and a tattoo of a dove just behind her ear that only certain people are allowed to see. People like the boy, who just dumped her, but definitely not her mom who would ground her for life. Ground her for a multitude of reasons such as: going against her wishes and getting the tattoo or for using fake ID to get into ' The Ukrainian Hall '.

The old woman also ignores the norms and encroaches into the woman's sphere of personal space. She stands rigidly, on one leg, and smiles at the woman who finally takes notice and steps back uncertainly.

"Do not waste your tears on the parched earth, It's so greedy!" the old woman smoothly commands.

The crying woman stares at the old woman both curious and untrusting. The old woman smiles alluringly and gently wipes away the young woman's tears with her bony fingers. She swirls her tongue around and around her own fingers savoring every molecule. The young woman is horrified and backs away into the deepening shadows.

"What the hell are you doing?" she demands of the older woman.

"Don't fret, dear. Just follow me and your sadness will disappear." the old woman coaxes.

She signals the young woman to follow as she leads the way back to the lake. The young woman hesitates, at first, but is soon swept along behind the stilted gait of the old woman as if drawn after her by some invisible cord.

They arrive at the lake - now darkened by thick heavy overcast skies.

The old woman gracefully slices into the briny water until the water licks at her waist. She turns and motions the young woman to follow. The young woman hesitates then slowly wades into the water to stand in front of the old woman who smiles and takes the young woman's hands in hers.

"This is the place where the first tears were shed by the first man and the first woman. They knew that holding back grief could result in illness of the body and the spirit. You must release it as our ancestors have done. Don't hold back! Release it now!"

The young woman pauses self-consciously and slightly embarrassed, but then a single tear comes. Then another and another and another until the tears stream down her face and she is racked with sobs and shakes and shudders. Blinded by her tears, the young woman doesn.t notice when the old woman releases her hands and strides out onto the shore. She looks back once, smiles and sighs, and then returns to the dusty road and walks away.

The young woman now consumed in her grief and wailing, also failed to notice that the water level of the lake has changed and has now risen to her breasts. Her tears fill the lake to brimming then overflowing! The salty brine rises and rises and swallows the young woman - silencing her wailing and her grief. The dark clouds rumble and slam together creating a shock wave that sweeps over the water rippling it - a thousand fold.

And then silence.

The water becomes still. The insects hushed and the clouds dissipate revealing a blood-orange night sky glowing with the suns final rays. The glassy surface of the lake is shattered as a white dove shoots out from the depths and soars into the bloody sky, high above the lake and out of sight.

The old woman lounges at the bar. She observes the other patrons who are already wasted or perhaps were never sober. Some mumble incoherently, some cry quietly to themselves. The old woman shakes her head and chuckles in amusement as she sips her Pernod on the rocks.

(Of course there's no Pernod in this backwater bar! But she makes do as she sips on a rye and seven.)

A monstrous man lumbers into the bar atop tree trunk-like legs. He's scruffy and dirty and sports a tee shirt which depicts a woman with gigantic breasts bending over in front of the camera and the caption reads, ' Got milk? '. His eyes reveal a hard-knock life of debauchery and jail time and they sparkle with mischief as he hunts for his prey.

The old woman perks up and sits tall on her bar stool. She senses the black energy emanating from the newly arrived redneck and she sniffs the air.

Said redneck hones in on a solitary, elderly Asian man dressed in an ancient thread bare suit. He sits, by himself, reading an old out-of-date Chinese newspaper. He seems to savor each word and the ice-cold beer which sweats by his elbow. The redneck ambles over to the Asian man's table, snatches the newspaper and crumples it into a ball and drops it on the table. The Asian man looks up incredulously, about to tear the offenders head off, but sees that flight might be the better option. He rises to leave but the redneck pushes him back down with a painful thud. The Asian man winces and cringes when the redneck grabs a fistful of his threadbare suit.

"Buy me a pitcher and I'll let you and your squinty chink eyes walk outta here!" the redneck bellows for all to hear.

The Asian man just nods and shakes with fear and hurriedly stumbles to the bar to secure his release.

"Hurry up slant-eyes, I'm mighty thirsty."

The other patrons shake their heads in disgust at the shocking display of senior abuse! But no one stops him and no one looks him in the eye - just as they did on the playground when tormented by the bullies, so many years ago.

The old woman, however, leers over her raised glass taking in every inch of the monstrous monster.

He notices and dismisses her with his hammy digits, "Don't bother ya old battle-axe, I'm not interested in a dried up old prune like you!"

The old woman grins hungrily, keeping her eyes on the brutish lout.

The terrified Asian man returns with the pitcher, trembling so hard that it sloshes vigorously and spills to the carpet.

(The same carpet that has covered the floor since the bar opened one hundred years ago and has drunk so much spilled alcohol - it's become addicted to the stuff. When it's very quiet in the bar and if you listen very carefully you can hear the carpet sing, ' How dry I am, how dry I am. ')

The bully grabs the pitcher with one huge hand and the Asian man with the other and pours the contents of the pitcher over the old man's head, completely soaking his prized suit. He sputters and coughs and adds his tears to his already wet face. The bully, belly laughs, thinking this scene hilarious and well worth his money which of course he didn't spend. He glares around the room daring anyone stupid enough to complain - to complain!

(No one dares.)

A few women and even a few men wipe tears from their own eyes feeling sorrow for the Asian man and their own lack of courage. Most patrons, however, sigh in relief, grateful it's someone else and hopeful this cruel act with sate the bullies urge for pain.

A ragged bar towel, yellow and stiff with spilled beer, falls over the old man's shoulders. He jumps, startled at the touch and the unexpected compassion. The old woman gently towels the old man off, cooing reassurance as she works. He begins to cry anew with equal measures of shame, humiliation and pleasure. He mutters words of thanks in Chinese and the old woman smiles and nods her head.

The bully, instead of feeling satisfaction, feels resentment at this old woman who has partially spoiled his fun! She will pay for this slight and it will be a pleasure to torment someone so old and helpless.

The old woman begins to lead the old man out of the bar and guides him by his elbow - sopping wet with beer. She turns slyly to make sure the bully watches her, lead the old man out, and knows that he will wait a few minutes before he follows - close on her heels. But for the first time in a very long time, her prediction proves false! So long, in fact, that the emotion is alien and new feeling. She likes this rebirthing of emotions even though it signals her fallibility. This bully is worthy of her attention and the challenge he now presents.

And while this is all going on in the woman's head, the bully has fixed his gaze on a new target. Two new targets in fact!

Mincing, nervously into the bar, is Paul, the only ' out ' person in the entire region and he appears to be searching for someone.

The bully is delighted, at this unexpected chain of events, and snatches a fresh pour right out of the bartenders nicotine-stained fingers. The bartender thinks about raising his voice to chastise the offender but realizes the folly of such an endeavor just in the nick of time.

Newcomer Paul, meanwhile, has located his date. Nervously fidgeting, at a secluded table, is handsome Dale. He's fit and tanned and scared to death as he experiences his first foray into online dating. Well, not really online dating, but mobile dating as Dale took the plunge and downloaded the ' splat.org ' app. The only person within 100 kilometers just happened to be the mincing Paul - now making his way over to Dale's table.

"Six pack my ass!" quips Dale to himself but beggars can't be choosers.

Two young horny men are hardly going to take issue with a few extra kilos, around the middle, and so they get right to sussing one another out and drinking.

A few older patrons, at the bar, make the limp wrist universal signal for ' gay ' and giggle to themselves but those who noticed the two men sitting close together, for the most part, just shrug and live and let live.

(But not so the bully of this tale.)

He has taken an avid interest in this hook-up date made possible from the fine folks at ' splat.org '! The bully, truth be told, is mildly aroused and a tiny bit jealous.

(Bully's, it is said, are gay men in denial of their repressed sexuality resulting in their anti-social behavior.)

(Does that mean bullies in the gay community are actually heterosexual?

A topic for another day!)

The bully, now sporting a noticeable bulge in the front of his filthy shorts, slowly and deliberately crashes over to the table of ' splat '. The two potential lovers ignore him, focusing their attention on each other instead.

On the way to the lake of tears, the Asian man sobs and blubbers in Chinese and the old woman feigns genuine concern. Her mind, though, is back at the bar marveling at the bully and what a prize he might become. A big man so full of sorrow, despair and depression – a great big water balloon about to burst!

Dale is just about to ask Paul, "Have you ever been given a blowjob by someone who kept their glasses on and did he... "

But just then the bully slams his paw down hard on their table and their beers dance about and spew every which way.

They both gawk at the size of the hand as the bully bellows, "Well lookie here, and not one but two homasexals!"

The spilled beer, dripping off the tabletop, is now the loudest sound in the bar as a hush has settled over everyone. They hold their breathes in fear of what may come next.

The carpet begins to sing, "How dry I..." but stops - sensing the gravity of the situation.

The silence is finally broken.

The bully holds the boys by the neck and squeezes vice-like, "What are ya waiting for? Don't ya wanna kiss like fags?"

The would be lovers try and shake their heads ' no ' but the bully holds them fast and then mashes their mouths together until blood begins to trickle down their chins. They moan in pain which excites the bully even more.

He addresses the bar, "Listen to em a moanin! Disgusting preverts!"

The bully pins Dale to the table with one tree-trunk leg and momentarily lets go of his neck. He guzzles some beer, uncaring how much dribbles down his soiled wife beater, down his substantial shit-belly and onto his barely concealed erection.

Every patrons knuckles are white as they clench their hands down on something hard – a glass, the tabletop, their other hand – waiting for the sadist to take the next step.

The old woman hurries down the dusty road, her mind dwelling on the bully. She wonders how many people he has tormented since she's been gone and what condition they might be in? A still dripping morning dove settles onto her shoulder, cooing sweet nothings in her tattooed ear.

"No need to thank me, just fly away now, I've got others to attend to," she snaps at the dove, annoyed.

"You're free, now get!" the old woman swats the dove into the air like a well-struck shuttlecock.

The dove flutters and hovers for a few uncertain moments then soars away, the old woman already forgotten.

"So, which one a you homos is the bender and which one is the one who bends over?" the bully queries, hands on hips in a very effeminate way.

The ' splatters ' massage their swollen mouths, rinse their mouths with beer and spit on the floor.

(Much to the appreciation of the ancient carpet.)

"Ain' t talkn? Well maybe I'll just bend ya both over and see which one a you likes it best!"

The would-be-lovers spring to their feet, determined to make the proverbial ' run-for-it '!

(And you would think that two young men, brimming with testosterone, could easily slip by a talking brontosaurus? Alas, this particular brontosaurus has rather long and powerful arms!)

The bully easily snags the young men by their necks and slams them onto the tabletop - slams their squashed faces against the table top with their butts exposed and vulnerable. The bully raises his head so he can gloat to the entire bar. His massive smile widens from ear to ear.

No one meets his eye!

But as he turns back to his squirming prey, pinned to the sticky tabletop, he notices a pair of spindly wizened legs in the periphery of his lusty vision. His smile contracts into a frown as he pans upward to meet the glare of the old woman standing stock still on one leg with her arms folded across her bony chest.

"You're a brave one, ya old hag!" he spits at her, "Ya like ta watch?"

The bully guffaws at his own cleverness but the old woman remains stoically silent and unmoving, waiting for her prey to swim into range.

Whether it's the presence of the old woman or it's just time to let go - the would-be-lovers begin to sob simultaneously. And to add to this very bizarre tableau of verisimilitude, the old woman and the bully grin and look at one another simultaneously but for very different reasons.

"I see you - you big oaf! I see you behind that big thick mask"; she coos and widens her grin to a smile.

The bully glares at her, pushing her back with his gaze.

The would-be-lovers are now mewling between sobs which makes the whole sordid scene even more surrealistic and uncomfortable.

"Why don't you let the young men go? They' re no good to you now. They're spent." the old woman asks politely.

The would-be-lovers stop their bawling and hold their breaths in hopefulness.

"If you need to pick on someone, pick on me!" she dares.

"But maybe you're just chicken " the old woman booms out for all to hear.

Eyebrows are raised incredulously!

The bully slowly shifts his facial features from gobsmacked to an uncertain grin.

"What fun could I have with you?" he spits, "You're an old and tough old bird. You're no match for me."

"Cluck, cluck, cluck" she mimics and taunts.

Gasps are released.

The bully loosens his grip on the young men but doesn't let them go. Even so, they relax a little bit and begin to breath normally.

The old woman smiles, "That's better. You show mercy. More than your father ever did."

The bully, unnerved by this unexpected direction, looks gravely at the old woman.

"Even when you cried out for him to stop, he didn't, did he?" she postulates.

The bully begins to sweat a bit, his oafish body triggered by memory. Not the heat of the day warm sticky sweat but the icy trickle of panic. The bully shifts uncomfortably on his massive legs.

"Even your siblings couldn't help you when you cried out. And when they came of an age, they joined in too!" she empathizes then chides, "All in the family?"

Breath is inhaled in shock and disbelief.

The bully backs up a step but still holds the young men down on the table.

"No," is all he can say, "that never happened."

"Dear oh dear, you know it did, Over and over and over again!" she purrs, "Not even God heard your screams! Hard to say which is worse, being victimized by your entire family or discovering that God doesn't care or answer prayers."

The bully slowly turns his enormous head from side to side.

"Daddy...My Pa was a good man. He..." the bully searches for the words but they hide behind the jittery film playing in his head.

The eight-millimeter reel that should show amateur camera work of a picnic or a visit to ' Disneyland ' or someone's long forgotten birthday. Instead it plays like a slick porn movie with horrid acting and stunningly detailed sex acts.

"Poor dear! It's all flooding back to you now. A giant wave pinning your face to the coarse beach sand. Pinning you down until your airs running out, pinning you down until the panic sets in." the old woman smiles in pity.

A single tear meanders down the bully's stubbly and pock marked face. The young men wince as grief clenches the bully's hands around their bruised necks and their faces flush with fresh blood.

The old woman lurches toward them in protective reflex. The bully takes no notice as he relives his childhood trauma.

"Let them go now. Please let the boys go." she urges but doesn't plead. "It's just you and me now, No need to include them. Show me that you are a better man than the men you knew." the old woman smiles.

The bully marvels at the old woman, as if she just materialized out of thin air. He cocks his head trying to comprehend this new reality.

His new reality.

The old woman uses her head to gesture to the two young men – the bully has pinned to the table.

He studies them, wondering how they got there and why he's the one crushing them. How they wriggle, like the various bugs and small animals he used to torment and squash to relieve his childhood misery.

Misery as a reaction to misery.

The bully winces and lets go of their necks as if electrocuted. He holds up his hands expecting burned and blistering flesh - like the burns from a cigarette. His hands, however, are untouched. He blows on them anyway.

The would be and might still be lovers rush to the old woman's side and tremble as she spreads her arms around them like wings. Their tears drip to the floor like a teasing rain shower in the desert – full of such promise but stingy with the delivery.

The old woman cringes inside with the thought of all that wasted water. But the prize before her is the mother lode and she's oh so close. So close - she can, in fact, taste it. The warm salty misery of the oafs traumatic past is perfection on her outstretched tongue. Her eyes roll back into her narrow head and she moans in anticipation.

In the mirror, behind the bar and tinged yellow by years of nicotine, the faces of the regulars and the bar flies look back, frozen in time. For time is at a standstill while the old woman and the bully face-off in this bizarre dance.

The bully, no longer anchored by the young men, tumbles back as if he were made of paper instead of hundreds of kilos of dense flesh. He doesn't notice as his momentum sends him careening through tables and chairs. He bowls over beer glasses and ashtrays that explode in his wake. And finally he crashes into a half wall - landing squarely on his ass. And there he sits just like he did as a young abused boy in a make-believe safe world of his own creation. A world where a loving father doesn't sodomize him or beat on him or sell his fine young ass for a bottle of rye and a carton of smokes.

But that world no longer exists for this big boy man.

Thirty-five-years of bubbling hissing lava memory is now surging to the surface. The molten memories seeking out weakened fissures to erupt high into the air.

The old woman studies the bully curling into himself and starting to rock back and forth in vulnerable re-assurance. He is ready she thinks to herself. He's ripe and juicy and ready to be plucked from the tree but she mustn't rush. No, now is the time for patience. Let out some more line and play him for a while before pulling him into the boat and clubbing him over the head.

What an interesting picture they make as they trundle down the dusty road crowded with growing shadows. The old woman stilting along more stiffly with each step, with one teary eyed young man under each wing. And trudging along behind her, one meaty paw clenching her robe, is the bully - eyes downcast and muttering to himself. He is towed along like a child helping his mother shop but not wanting to be there. He kicks up clouds of choking dust that blacken his face when the dust mixes with his tangy tears.

Standing on the lake edge, the probably - will be lovers gasp at the beauty stretching out before them. The old woman grins as she joins their appreciation for the glowing crimson lake which mirrors the giant sinking sun as it burns into the horizon. The three of them slip into the viscous yet silky water, the young men unresisting and wading out quite willingly.

The old woman snaps to a stop with the realization that the young men are no longer in misery and more importantly their tears no longer drip into the lake.

"Why have you stopped crying? What's wrong?" the old woman croaks.

The young men gaze pityingly at the bully who has plopped down in the mud at the edge of the lake.

"We feel sorry for him." they both say in unison, "His childhood must have been horrid!"

The old woman crinkles her face in annoyance and dismay, "After all the rotten things he did to you, why aren't you traumatized?"

The young men entwine hands and shrug and Dale says, "Most messed up first date I've ever been on. It's got to be down hill from now on."

Paul chimes in, "Smooth sailing!"

The old woman spits as the young men wade away from her and further out into the deep water where they begin to swim and cavort.

The resilience of youth is what she might have said in her inside voice but instead she uses her outside voice to moan, "Spoil sports."

Cutting gracefully through the water, like a flamingo, the old woman closes in on the bully. He tries to come to terms with his non-bully status and his washed clean memories of childhood assault. He hugs himself tightly, as he wallows in the salty mud, eyes firmly shut.

The old woman clears her dry and reedy throat and waits. The non-bully turns his giant head from side to side in an emphatic and childish ' NO '.

"Come on now. I can stand here all day and wait. Open your eyes and face me. I'm not going to hurt you. In fact I intend to help you, if you'll let me." she promises.

"NO!" the non-bully defies and even nods his head emphatically.

The old woman clucks at his insolence. He opens his eyes, curiously, and seeing her displeasure begins to slither away through the muck like a python that's swallowed a whole, still kicking and squirming, child. Even though his escape attempt is comical at best, the old woman shoots out her bony arm with lightning speed and grabs the non-bully in a crushing grip by his ankle. The non-bully writhes around, like a rabbit caught cruelly in a leg hold trap, screaming out in imagined agony.

The old woman laughs, at his futile antics, as she slowly tows him into the briny lake water. His agonized exaggerated screams turn into gurgles of realized panic as he fights to keep his nose and mouth out of the salty lake. The old woman glides to a stop when the water reaches her waist - then lets the non-bully go. He surges to his feet gasping and gagging on the water of the lake and at the same time manages to glare at the old woman.

"You almost drownded me, you old cow!" he coughs.

"And yet you've prayed for release many times." she responds serenely.

He just gawks at the old woman, dumbfounded, until the rage ebbs and his limbs no longer shake.

"Give me your hands!" she commands.

"Why?" he argues.

"I said my intention was to help you, so give me your hands." she demands.

Whether it's her piercing eyes or the tone of her voice or perhaps he's just exhausted, but this time he complies. And there they stand far out into the saline lake, his hulking form towering over her fragility and yet she controls the proceedings.

"This is the place where the first tears were shed by the first man and the first woman. They knew that holding back grief could result in illness of the body and the spirit. You must release it as our ancestors have done. Don.t hold back! Release it now!"

The non-bully raises his substantial eyebrows, wondering if he heard the old woman correctly. Surely a right bastard like himself is not meant to cry like a baby in the middle of a dead lake in rural Saskatchewan?

She reads his thoughts, "Yes you are! And yes you will."

The bully, once again, tries to shake free of the old woman's grip but she holds fast - like an eagles talons on the flopping head of a spawning salmon.

"Remember how much it hurt that first time? You couldn't sit properly for a week. Remember?" she draws out the memories.

The non-bully clenches his teeth, "It always hurt!"

"That's it! Now we're getting somewhere. Remember the shame! The betrayal? How could he? How could they? You trusted them! Family is supposed to look out for one another!" she pushes him until he teeters.

The first tears begin to well just behind his big cow eyes which slowly begin to bulge out.

"Daddy…" is all he can manage as the damn breaks.

The old woman smiles and releases her grip to a more gentle and supportive one.

 "There's no one here to see you, my son. Let it all go, it's just you and me." she whispers.

The non-bully begins to gasp between choking sobs. All his buried grief comes out way too fast for his battered body to process.

The old woman gently lays a palm on his chest, "Breathe. Just slow down and breathe, you'll be alright. "

Slowly, the non-bully relaxes and his breathing slows. At the same time a lifetime of pent-up tears begin to roar down his face and spill into the lake. The non-bully's face is a mess. Salty tears from his eyes, snot from his nose and drool roll freely as he breathes from his mouth. He is oblivious to his surroundings and blinded by his torrent of rushing tears. He doesn't notice the old woman as she glides into deeper water singing an ancient but familiar tune.

The brine washes over her head and she disappears into the depths.

The non-bully releases his grief into the greedy lake which has already risen to his broad shoulders and still he weeps. A weeping that is now in control of this man-boy slowly disappearing into the lake. A weeping that is deeply spiritual right down to the level of the soul and a weeping that will re-align this once bully into a new man.

Dark clouds rumble and slam together - creating a shock wave that sweeps over the water rippling it a thousand fold.

And then silence.

The water becomes still. The insects hushed and the clouds dissipate revealing a crimson night sky glowing with the suns final rays.

The glassy surface of the lake is shattered as a white owl surges from the depths and soars into the bloody sky, high above the lake and out of sight.

The surface of the lake is broken again by the emergence of the non-bully waddling like a huge goose. He is no longer grieving, no longer weeping. He is serene and determined as he makes his way toward shore. He clumsily makes his way to the dusty road and as he moves along, his awkward waddling becomes more human.

On the dusty road, the non-bully begins to stride along with determination and purpose.

He is indeed a new man and much more.

His bare feet kick up the dust and when he glimpses ' The Ukrainian Hall ' in the distance, he smiles. And his smile widens when he wonders, in his huge head, if today might be the day his father decides to wet his whistle? Or perhaps his uncle? Or one of his brothers?

The End

DOUBLE DOG DARE

"I can't see anything!" Jimmy whines and snorts in disgust as the syrupy fog obscures his view.

Even at nine-years-old Jimmy is a dapper young man with shades and a fedora and facial expressions more suited to someone middle-aged

"Can we get ice cream there?" his twin sister Jill pleads.

Jill is quite feminine and feline with shoulder length blond hair. Whereas Jimmy clomps around on two big flat feet, Jill spends most of her time on tiptoe and flits around like a faerie.

"Be patient." their father Ellis placates.

Ellis is tall and muscular and Jimmy frequently reminds him, his thinning hair is going grey.

"No ice cream! No chocolate! No candy!" laughs their mom, Breanne.

Breanne holds them all together with confident authority. She would like to do more sporty activities, with the other three, but her knee is as they say - a bum!

"Awww!" the twins bawl in unison which after nine years is still disconcerting but not as much as when they converse, with one another. while sleeping

"There's no stores, you idiots! We told you - this is a birding tour and we might go to the lighthouse museum." Breanne informs her children.

"We never get to do what we want!" Jill sulks not garnering any sympathy from either parent or her twin brother. Jimmy has found the orange whistle on his PFD and is now annoying everyone else on the boat and not just his parents.

A few far away answering whistles and Jimmy and Jill soon discover that another set of twins are onboard and seem to be as bored as they are.

"Can we go see those other kids?" Jimmy asks.

Ellis reasonably says, "What did the Captain say when we got onboard?"

"Stay in your assigned seats," the twins reply.

"And why?" prompts Breanne.

They both slouch and exhale their reply, "Because there have been over 160 shipwrecks off Seal Island and he doesn't want to be 161!"

"OMG! You actually listened this time!" Breanne sarcastically points out.

The tour guide, a young female university student from Dartmouth wearing flip-flops, a tee and shorts, shivers in the clammy fog. She helps the tour passengers disembark and apologizes for the foul weather but hopes it may clear up.

Most of the tour is made up of German tourists who just nod or smile at the guide's words. The men curse in German among themselves about their luck, the weather and lack of beer. They wear football shirts and jeans and the ladies are all decked out in khaki everything. *(Must have made a stop at Tilley Endurables or MEC)*

Once they are all safely off the boat and milling about the West side wharf, the guide addresses the group.

"So just a few words before I turn you loose. The lighthouse museum is open and feel free to go check it out anytime you want. This is not a guided tour but I will be around of course to help you identify the multitude of species on the island. You are free to explore the entire island – just make sure you stay clear of the shore as this is one of the most dangerous bodies of water in the East Coast with crazy tides and currents. And on a day like this visibility is limited so be careful. Have fun exploring and don't worry about getting lost as it's a tiny island and we'll find you. Let's meet back here in five hours."

The Germans stand still, expectantly waiting for a translation that never comes. The guide finally shoes them off the wharf like a gaggle of geese and they get their cameras and birding books and meander away.

Jill and Jimmy have made fast friends of Claire and Eugene Crowells as is the way of nine-year-olds. The foursome venture out on their own after stern safety warnings from all four parents. The Crowells twins have dark black hair and are much more squat and round compared to Jimmy and Jill who are quite thin and blond.

The sun tries desperately to burn off the dragon's breath but it seems determined to ruin the Germans day and conceal parts of the tiny island from all the intruders. All intruders, except the Crowells twins, who are direct descendants of the first settlers of Seal Island. Though that bit of history has been lost, as generations have cared less and less. Back in the day, they would have been known as the East siders, a rather proud bunch with no fear of the surrounding waters. Which probably resulted in the reduction of family numbers and the increase of shipwreck numbers.

The twin twins decide to race to the Blond Rock end of the island as they've heard about the multitude of ships that ran aground there and the many drowning's.

"Maybe we'll see a ghost?" Eugene wonders out loud.

Jimmy, a firm skeptic at age nine of anything magic and paranormal, rolls his bright eyes and says, "Ya, right!"

Out of breath but finally warmed up, the four children stop to get their bearings. They should be quite close to Blond Rock but the fog is viscous and visibility is extremely poor. When they look back the way they came, they see the hot sun bathing the rest of the island which the Germans are taking advantage of. They hurriedly remove breathable outer layers to expose sandals with sport socks, white undershirts and a plethora of sagging pasty skin.

"Gross!" Jimmy and Jill exclaim as Eugene and Claire laugh.

The four momentarily forget about the unnatural weather pattern that hangs heavily over them.

"Have you heard about the Pig Man?" Claire asks Jimmy and Jill who shake their heads negatively.

"If you stand in front of a mirror and say ' Here piggy, piggy, pig, pig, pig ' three times in a row, he'll appear and slit your throat!" Claire says slyly, checking to see if her brother smiles, and he does.

"I haven't heard of that one." Jill admits a bit uncertainly and wondering where the conversation may be going and who these Crowells twins really are?

"Have you tried it?" Jimmy asks daringly.

Eugene pipes in, "Naw, we saw it on American Horror Story."

"What's that?" Jill and Jimmy ask in sync.

The Crowells twins gasp in shock and roll their eyes, "You don't watch American Horror Story?"

Jill and Jimmy shrug.

Claire confides, "We watch it when Grandma babysits and falls asleep."

Jill and Jimmy, "Cool!"

Claire pulls out a small powder-blue make-up mirror, holds it up to her face, smiles and recites, "Here piggy, piggy, pig, pig, pig!"

Jill's jaw drops and she takes a step back.

Jimmy, giggling uncontrollably, grabs the mirror and holds it up to his face and recites, "Here piggy, piggy, pig, pig, pig!"

Eugene is about to recite the final incantation and reaches for the mirror but Jill beats him to it. She snatches it from Jimmy's hand and runs into the deep fog.

Jill finds herself standing on the damp rocks and pebbles near Blond Rock. It's low tide and she is buffeted by a howling Southwest gale. She shivers and holds herself tight as the wind tries to pry her loose and lift her off her freezing sandaled feet. The ambient light has changed drastically and all the color has washed out as if she was transported back in time to a black and white film. Jill tries to yell for her brother but the din of the gale muffles her voice to a mere whisper-level. The rocks and pebbles, beneath her, begin to vibrate and shift and she turns seaward just in time as a massive steam ship grates across the rock and runs-a-ground. The sound of metal scraping and scouring over the rocks permeates her teeth and bones and she falls to her knees and tries to block out the sound with her hands. A gapping hole has been rent on the starboard side of the ship and the rising tide slowly begins to lap at the hole as if deciding if it's worth filling up. Jill gazes up at the ships hull which reads ' SS Ottawa '. She can just make out the small figure of a woman, long black hair and a high collared white dress, waving to her from the rusted deck. The woman remains calm as if her ship running a ground was a mere inconvenience. From a distance, the woman looks very pale as if the color were washed out of her as well. Jill waves back tentatively but the act frightens her as if some invisible line has been crossed.

Jimmy, Claire and Eugene spread out and search for Jill who is either doing a very good job of hiding and scaring the crap out of the other children or she's vanished into thin air. When she ran into the fog she appeared to have winked out of existence.

"Jill!" they all call repeatedly and to no avail.

The three meet up again at roughly the same place that Jill is currently standing and if they occupied the same space and time - they could reach out and touch her.

Jimmy wipes sweat from his brow with the back of his hand. The weather has become hot and humid like the rest of the island. The odd fog seemed to have shrunk in size when it swallowed his sister, "Where did she go? This is just weird!"

Eugene and Claire concur and, for emphasis, shrug.

The sound of Jill's name swirls around her as if coming from every direction at once and her head spins as she tries to visually follow the sound. Her name swirls around and around her faster and faster and she soon gets dizzy and begins to swoon. Just before she faints completely, she notices that the gaunt woman is no longer on the deck of the ship.

Jimmy, Claire and Eugene, intrigued by the sound of someone moaning, look down and find Jill shivering and bluish curled up at their feet and hyper-ventilating.

Claire bends down and gently rubs Jill's shoulder.

"What happened?" she asks with genuine concern.

Jill slowly gets up and wipes blood and sand away from her abraded knees as the other children support her and help her up. Jill, still clutching the mirror in one small hand, returns it to Claire who smiles.

"I was lost in the fog. I couldn't see you guys and everything was black and white and cold. A big metal ship ground up on the rocks," she points, "and it was called the SS Ottawa and a lady waved to me."

Jimmy, the skeptic, just says, "Wait. What?"

Eugene and Claire look at one another in fear and surprise.

Eugene exclaims, "She saw Annie!"

Claire nods but she's enrapt with the mirror that Jill has returned. When she looks at her own reflection, it's not in sunlit glorious color but washed out black and white and the background is rolling fog. She's about to show everyone else when Annie's bloodless corpse walks behind her with an eerie grin directed at Claire. Claire SCREAMS and hurls the mirror onto the beach which shatters into countless tiny fragments.

Grabbing hold of his shaking twin sister, Eugene asks consolingly, "What is it Claire? What did you see? Did you see her too?"

Jimmy barges in, "Who's she? I thought we were trying for the Pig Man?"

Eugene gives his sister a hug, which causes Jimmy to roll his eyes, and leads her to an old and weathered wooden lifeboat. It's been turned over to keep the rain out. He has her sit down and lean her back against the boat. Jimmy sighs and begrudgingly helps his own twin sister to the boat and sits her beside Claire. The girls remain silent and just stare into space trying to absorb the strange events unfolding in front of them and at a seemingly accelerating pace.

Eugene studies the battered old boat looking for any clue as to where the boat came from and who the owner might be, Jimmy joins him and they scour the hull for any identifying mark.

Jimmy stops his scanning and looks up, eyes ablaze, "I think I found a letter!"

Eugene comes closer and they use their bare hands to remove some encrusted sand to reveal the letters 'SS O '.

Eugene is excited and let's, "HOLY SHIT! " slip out before he swiftly checks his surroundings for parents and other grown-up party-poopers.

The girls snap out of it, alarmed at his expletive indiscretion that may impact them by association.

The children all crowd around the new discovery and Claire wonders, "SS Ottawa?"

Jill is unnerved by the thought and hugs herself, remembering the black and white world or dimension she just fell out of and the grating sound of the ship running a ground.

Jimmy, *(so skeptical he would have given James Randi a run for his money)*, looks quizzically at Eugene and Claire, "Oh c'mon, it could be anything! SS Otter, SS Orange, SS OMG!" he laughs at his own wit and even Jill manages a smile.

"It's Ottawa and you know it! This is the spot where she ran aground and your own sister just saw Annie!" trumpets Eugene proudly.

Jill garners some courage and asks, "So, who is Annie, anyway?"

On the other side of the island, Breanne and Ellis luxuriate in the silence of no children and sunbath in the tall grass. They don't talk, but they do hold hands, as they peer up at the ever-changing clouds and daydream about doing more of the same in seven or eight years. Breanne has it all calculated down to the exact days and hours and if she were able to book plane tickets seven years in advance - she would have done so. As a cloud changes from a pug to a wiener dog, she wonders if the German tourist call them wiener dogs too?

Ellis, grinning from ear to ear beside his wife, also thinks about the Germans except he is imagining them trying their hands at the chicken dance but dressed as SS Officers!

"...and she still walks the shoreline looking for survivors to this day." Eugene finishes the tale.

Jill hugs herself even tighter and tears well in her eyes at the thought of Annie waving to her from the doomed ship. Claire is in a similar state having seen Annie in the mirror and the way she smiled right at her -as if marking her.

Jimmy smiles and nods his head approvingly and says, "Good story! Too bad there wasn't a way to call her!"

"There is!" Eugene crows but winces as Claire punches his shoulder with considerable force, previously unfelt by Eugene.

"Don't!" she warns her twin brother - who is now thinking twice about tormenting her in the future.

"Spit it out!" Jimmy taunts Eugene, "Nothings going to happen!"

"I want to go back to Mom and Dad." Jill demands and Claire adds, "Ya, me too!"

Eugene regains some of his swagger buoyed by Jimmy - his new guy friend, "Then go, ya fraidy cats. Me and Jimmy will raise Annie from the dead and learn all her secrets!"

"Of course we will." Jimmy laughs and then uncharacteristically adds, "You go ahead sis, you've had a rough day. I'll be there shortly after Annie doesn't show!"

He grins at Eugene who grins back.

"Oh, you'll see!" Eugene promises.

"I'm going with Jill! See you later!" Claire says and grabs Jill by the hand and begins to lead her down the shoreline away from the boys.

Jill needs no coaxing and they pick up speed with each step they take.

The boys finish their work – a rough approximation of a mirror that they have cobbled together and laid out on the pebbles. Eugene motions for Jimmy to kneel beside him in front of the pseudo-mirror as if kneeling in front of an idol - like the Easter Islanders must have done or the Catholics! They gaze into the mirror shards which reflect nothing more than a kaleidoscope of their expectant faces.

"Annie, Annie, Annie – your flesh so cold, cold, cold

Annie, Annie, Annie – covered with mold, mold, mold

Annie, Annie, Annie – your lifeboat rolled, rolled, rolled!" recites Eugene who holds his breath.

Jimmy looks on impatiently and looks up and down the beach for something more interesting. And he finds it! Seal Island is almost entirely bathed in warm sunshine with the exception of a small patch of dense fog that rolls in the direction the girls were walking in. He's about to alert Eugene when he hears Eugene scream.

The girls initial relief of leaving the boys and, hopefully, Annie behind, is short-lived. They didn't notice, at first but now realize, that the faster they seemingly walked away from Blonde Rock - brought them closer to Blonde Rock. It's as if they're walking on some kind of surreal sidewalk that Esher might have dreamed up or a consultant at Pearson International! They look back at their twin brothers who seem to be praying in front of the derelict lifeboat. Their images were clear at first but now seem to be obscured by an odd fog that rolls off the water and swirls around them. It's clammy and cold and smells like rotting meat – much stronger than the usual ocean-side rot odor. Jill and Claire shiver and put an arm around one another for more than shared warmth.
Jill can barely make out Claire's face and pleads, "What's happening?"
As she waits for a meaningful and reassuring response from Claire, she notices the color draining from her face turning into a sickly black and white.

Eugene scurries away from the mirror and lifeboat like a lizard then collapses in on himself accompanied by his shuddering sobs.

"Eugene?" Jimmy slowly approaches his new friend wary of whatever has made Eugene react in such a powerful way.

"Eugene? Did you see something? Did you see Annie?" Jimmy asks with some concern and momentarily swallowing his skepticism.

Eugene just shakes his head in response making his tears fly in every direction. Jimmy wonders if he should console Eugene with a hug but is not quite sure of all the guy friend protocols as he is only nine and newly indoctrinated.

> *In case of a crying guy friend…?*
> *Punch him?*
> *Console him?*
> *Console and punch him?*
> *Get nearest grown-up, mother preferred over father?*
> *Run away!*

Jimmy leans heavily toward the runaway *(retreating)* option and is just about to act upon it when he notices Eugene has stopped sobbing and is staring at the lifeboat.

"I saw them." Eugene says to the lifeboat.

"Who?" prompts relieved Jimmy, "Who did you see?"

Eugene turns his head slowly to look at Jimmy much like a praying mantis.

He looks deep into Jimmy's eyes and says, "Claire and Jill."

Jimmy looks quizzically at Eugene, "What?"

"Claire and Jill" he repeats, "They were in the black and white world!"

Eugene, ignores the look of dread on Jimmy's face, turns his gaze to the lifeboat, "They were terrified!"

Clap, clap, clap clap!
Ducka, ducka, ducka, duck, ducka, ducka, ducka duck, ducka, ducka, ducka, duck duck duck! Ellis sings in his head.

His chicken dancing Gestapo fantasy is abruptly interrupted by Breanne who suddenly sits up and scans three hundred and sixty degrees and observes, "It's too quiet!"

Begrudgingly, Ellis sits up and looks around knowing that he won't see or hear his children as Breanne's ' my children are in or causing trouble ' radar is much more attuned than his own.

"Call them or catch them in the act?" she smiles at Ellis.

He smiles back and replies, "Catch them. I wouldn't mind exploring the island a bit and I'm stiff from lying in the grass for so long."

Breanne nods and collects their things and hand in hand they begin to roam.

The boys, visibly shaken and scared, scan the mirror glass for any signs of their twins. The mirror world is worse than Jill described. Absolutely everything from the sky to the shoreline and the ocean are completely drained of color. The ocean water looks black and viscous and sinister as the waves rush into the broken hull of the SS Ottawa. Except for the rolling of the ocean, they see no life as if everything in that world were dead or in the process of dying.

In the cloying fog, Jill looses sight and sound of Claire. She calls out, but the fog acts as a baffle and no sound comes out. In a blind panic, Jill surges off, in the direction she last saw Claire, stumbling over unseen pebbles and wet rocks, her arms outstretched before her like a blind-girl. Claire mimics Jill's panic and sprints in the direction she last saw Jill, desperately trying to locate her new friend and get out of the dead world. As it turns out, both Claire and Jill are running in the same direction only a meter apart. Unfortunately, their normally quite good sense of direction has let them down as they now race for the dead worlds vitriolic sea.

Breanne and Ellis joyfully meander around Seal Island enjoying their alone time and not giving a second thought to the bird sighting checklist now crushed in the bottom of one of their backpacks.

"Shall we head to Bon Rock where all the shipwrecks happen?" Breanne wonders aloud.

Ellis chuckles and corrects her, "Blonde Rock, my dear!"

Breanne snorts and swats at her husband playfully, "You and your trivial mind! I suppose you have all the dates and names of the shipwrecks memorized!"

Ellis' face turns a shade red that resembles a slight sunburn, "Maybe." he confesses.

Breanne laughs, "I knew it! Nerd!"

Ellis sneers mockingly but good naturedly, then points to the shoreline in the distance, "That looks like our boy and his new friend but I don't see the girls."

Breanne shrugs, "Probably sick of the male bonding and posturing and off doing their own thing."

The ground beneath Claire and Jill falls away and they pinwheel their limbs trying to compensate. The distance from the small drop-off they have just run over is quite small in relative terms, say three meters. In dead world terms and not being able to see - it feels like an eternity of falling. Falling, falling, falling and then the freezing slap of the black sea! The force, surprise and immersion in the icy sheet of water jolts their bones and drives the wind out of their lungs like getting hit by a soccer ball in the breadbasket. The girls gasp for air but suck in the freezing brine in its place. Submerged and not knowing which way is up, they thrash and flay and try to cough out the salty water which burns their throats. Their feet are grasped by bony claws that dig deep into the skin and begin to reel in the girls - pulling them down toward the bottom.

(And sometimes that's all it takes to motivate someone!)

As if on cue, Jill and Claire kick with all their might using previously untapped reserves of energy and adrenaline. It's not that the girls know where the surface and life-sustaining oxygen is - it's just that they will explore any alternative direction to the monsters that are pulling them in the opposite direction.

The nine-year-olds kick and kick and kick again and manage to free their feet and begin to rise. They've run out of air long ago but the adrenaline, coursing through them, pushes them the last meter or so to the black rolling surface.

Jimmy and Eugene monitor the broken mirror like air traffic control radar operators trying to keep the teeming multitudes of aircraft from crashing into one another.

The boys gasp as they watch Claire and Jill break the surface of the dead ocean far out from shore and close to the stern of the SS Ottawa. They look on helplessly as Jill and Claire sputter and cough and upchuck the black goo of the sea. The girls tread water and try to orient themselves looking around madly. At last, they see one another and grab ahold.

Jimmy, the ex- skeptic cries, "What are we going to do, we have to help them!"

He studies the shoreline for answers.

"What can we do? They're in a different place!" Eugene responds holding up his hands in futility.

Jimmy scampers over to the lifeboat, "What about this? It's from that time!"

"Maybe, if we can get it out to them, they'll see it and if they can see it they can use it!" adds Eugene.

"Look!" Jimmy points ocean ward. A small patch of dense fog has formed not far from Blonde Rock but in deeper water.

The boys fly into action and try and lift the lifeboat. Its too heavy and they're only nine with undeveloped boys bodies. They heave on one side and right the boat. Jimmy finds a scrap of rope still tied to the bow and he grips it with both hands as Eugene hurries to the stern to push.

"One, two, three!" the boys count in unison.

Jimmy strains, leaning backwards and pulling with all his might. Eugene puts his shoulder into it like an ear-biting rugby player in a scrum. The boat scrapes along the dry rocks a centimeter at a time but soon begins to glide along, as the boys strain to maneuver it into the tidal rocks covered in green slime.

Teeth chattering, Claire and Jill catch movement out of the corner of their eyes and look up at the carcass of the SS Ottawa. Annie leans over the rusted and corroded railing and blows them kisses from her blackened lips. Jill and Claire cling to one another a little bit tighter. Some of the ships crew, worm-eaten flesh barely adhering to their yellow bones, jump off the ship deck - reliving the fateful night that she ran aground. They fall to the earth, like ducks peppered with shot on the first day of duck hunting season, hoping that the sea will cushion their fall.

But the sea has receded and only the stern is immersed in the inky black. The bodies smash onto the rocky shore, bones shattering with brittle snaps and entrails smacking and exploding. A ghastly stench hangs in the air and creeps along the ground and matte surface of the sea. Claire and Jill retch and swallow back bile, trying to breathe through their mouths still salty and sore from the languid brine.

The girls are so entranced, with the macabre scene unfolding before them, that they don't notice the bony gnarled fingers that slowly break the surface all around them. The long dead digits reach and stretch searching for something warm and living to join their ranks under the murky water.

(You see Blonde Rock has been claiming lives long before humans began to record time and events. The pairs of hands rising to the surface don't number in the 10's or even 100's. No, the rock has claimed 1000's with two more shortly to be added to the multitude.)

An entrepreneur from the 1800 's clamps on to Claire's left foot and tugs her down sputtering while a young shield maiden locks onto Jill.

The boys, meanwhile, are making good progress and are already ankle deep in the cold surf. They take an unannounced breather and lean on the boat, exhausted, and try to slow their inhalations. Jimmy gets up first and joins Eugene at the stern and together they heave the lifeboat past the breaking waves. The sea accepts the old boat and propels it farther out into the deeper water and eventually it disappears, swallowed up by the fog patch. Jimmy and Eugene smile in satisfaction and slop through the shallow water back to the shore. When they establish their footing again on the dryer pebbles, they race up to the makeshift mirror to determine if their plan has succeeded or not. Before them the dank dead sea rolls and froths with no sign of life.

"Where are they?" Eugene wonders.

Jimmy doesn't say anything, more worried for his sister than he ever thought was possible. He scans each shard of glass over and over again trying to find their lost twins.

Eugene shouts, "YES!" and points to the outermost shards.

Coming into view is the raggedy old lifeboat. In the world that the boys currently occupy, the lifeboat looked quant with its faded and flaking paint and weathered wood. Something someone, who lived in the top penthouse of a downtown Toronto condominium, might put on their rooftop garden to impress the unimpressionable.

But in the world that the girls occupy it looks foreboding, floating atop the dark churning water - empty.

The murk of the sea prevents Claire from seeing what has grabbed her foot and perhaps that' s a small mercy. The entrepreneur is no more than a jaundiced skeleton covered in mold and sickly vegetation. His jaw has long since detached as has his left arm and thus the reason he only clings to Claire with one bony hand.

Claire, quite acrobatic and flexible, curls into a ball so she can use her hands to extricate herself from the shipwreck victim from the 1800's. She feels rather than sees the claw like hand, wrapped around her foot and begins to pry off one finger at a time. A very dark version of ' he loves me, he loves me not! ' Claire disables the hand in mere seconds and charges to the surface.

Jill is having a harder time of it. Both her legs are in the grip of the shield maiden. *(and we all know there are no powder-puff Vikings!)* This particular shield maiden must have been very fond of Aegir as she is astonishingly well preserved. Jill knows this because every time she attempts to pry the offending fingers off, her own fingers encounter the shield maidens flesh - still attached. Jill searches her chilled brain for answers realizing that the prying is doing no good at all. And Jill, like all nine-year-old girls with their sweet facades but rather warped imaginations, comes up with a plan. If the hands won't pry loose then perhaps the arms will. Thanking her father for making her go to karate, Jill manages an underwater scissors kick and the resulting torque pulls the shield maidens arms from her sockets. The shield maidens smile turns into a grimace as she falls to the sea bottom while her arms and hands, still attached to Jill, rise to the surface.

Eugene kneels on the ground, in front of the reassembled mirror, eyes darting from shard to shard trying to find his sister. Jimmy stands directly behind him and hunched over with his hands resting on Eugene' s shoulder intent on sighting his own twin. Jimmy points to the right as Claire grabs the rail of the lifeboat and hauls herself in where she coughs and holds her chest. A moment later, Jill rockets out of the ocean like a breaching porpoise and seems to be screaming at Claire and pointing to her legs. The boys can't quite make it out but something is attached to her legs at the ankles. The girls work frantically but mostly unseen as all the action is taking place in the boats hull - blocked from view by the sides of the boat. Claire holds up two long ' I ' shaped objects and pitches them overboard in obvious disgust. Whatever they are, they seem to be alive as they thrash about on the water's surface like a non-sea bird with waterlogged wings. The objects try and climb up the boats hull but Claire and Jill carefully kick them off and the objects slip under the water's surface.

"They're safe!" Jimmy breaths a sigh of relief as the girls sit down in the lifeboat and finally enjoy a respite from the nightmare in the washed out world.

The boys stand up and study the fog patch, surreptitiously wiping a tear or two out of their eyes and hoping their new best guy friend doesn't pick, that exact moment to turn and look at them.

Ellis and Breanne have forgotten about Jill and Jimmy momentarily as they stroll along the small island enjoying the sounds and the smells and most of all each others company. Although they have been meandering, they've made steady progress toward Blonde Rock.

Close-by, the German's - now horribly sunburned, are getting into the flow of this bird=watching activity and their scorecards have quite a few species checked off. But not all the German's have their hearts in it! A few of the men, probably close to keeling over from heat stroke, are thinking about the next football match. Namely Bayern Munich's, and whether new Canadian wonder kid, Alphonso Davies will start and play the full ninety minutes. Okay, all of the men are only pretending to be interested in the birds and are really thinking about football and the liquid that goes so well with football – beer! So thirsty in the heat, on this Godforsaken island, with no bar and no television!

(But aside from all that, not the Germans nor Ellis and Breanne could imagine what happened next!)

From the direction of Blonde Rock echoes the cacophony of shrieking and frightened birds! Not just one or two birds but thousands! And In fact the entire Seal island avian population has taken flight and seem to be flying away as fast as they can from Blonde Rock. The sky is blackened with their multitude and the Germans, Ellis and Breanne duck for cover, even though the birds are hundreds of meters in the air.

Jill and Claire take a much-needed break to rest and collect their thoughts. If only the sun would make an appearance, they could get warm and get their clothes dry. More importantly, then they could see where they are. The fog is still quite thick and disorienting.

Claire offers, "We must be in deep water! Those things seemed to descend after we shook them off."

Jill nods looking down at the darkening finger-like bruise marks around her ankles. She imagines they must be blue but in this horrific world they are just a sickly black and gradations there of. A chill breeze picks up and pushes some of the fog out of the way. The girls observe that they are in deeper water, near the stern of the ghost ship, SS Ottawa. They scan the deck railings and ocean around them

but see no sign of fleshless ghouls or Annie -
seemingly the queen ghoul.

"How did the lifeboat get here? It totally saved
our butts!" Jill exclaims.

"Don't know. The boys maybe?" Claire
responds.

The chill breeze turns into a howling gale as if
all the souls who perished on Blonde Rock, exhaled
all at once.

*(No small feat considering their lack of organs,
namely lungs!)*

The oily water that surrounds the lifeboat
begins to churn with the wind and small waves
begin to bob the boat and the girls up and down.
The girls hold on to the rails, to keep their balance,
hoping they never have to enter the watery
graveyard again.

Jimmy and Eugene linger at the waters edge.
They gaze seaward in search of any signs or clues
as to the wellbeing of their twin sisters. They don't
speak but continue a silent vigil and promise to be
better brothers if their sisters make it back.

The wind on the water picks up and cools the
sweaty foreheads of the boys. The brothers who
have toiled long and hard hoping their actions have
made a difference in the colorless and lifeless
world. The breeze strengthens and the boys briefly
glance at each other with hope, as the fog begins to
blow out and burn off in the suns rays. Silence!
Complete and utter silence except for the sound of
the waves beginning to crash harder and more
frequently against their feet and legs.

No insect sounds, no birds or mammals!

Breaking their perfect camouflage of tree branches and holes in the earth and the detritus from the sea - all manner of bird take flight simultaneously and blacken the sky. The thrum of their wings-beats is deafening and their terrified shrieking - pecks it's way under the boys skin! The boys dive to the slick pebbles to avoid the frantic fowl, not caring or thinking about puncturing or scraping their own skin. The birds swirl, swoop and dive together and then surge away from Blonde Rock and soar south over Seal Island.

In the dead world, the fog has completely cleared. Jill and Claire cling to the rocking lifeboat threatening to capsize at any moment. The seas roar and hiss, all about them, and the bleak sky fills with heavy black clouds. Clouds that roll and crash together sending reverberations and shock waves through every fiber of the girls.
"I CAN'T HOLD ON!" Claire shouts at Jill.
Jill can't hear a word due to the din of the storm but gets the gist of Claire's message. She nods and points to shore then grabs the rail again as another whitecap smashes the lifeboat. Claire nods knowing that swimming for shore will be the only option should they tip over.

Eugene and Jimmy look out over the water, uncomprehending, as the seemingly empty lifeboat rocks madly from port to starboard, from bow to stern in the growing invisible storm. A sight made even more surreal by the fact that it's still a beautiful sunny day with clear skies and the only turbulence on the sea is in the immediate vicinity of the lifeboat!.

Ellis brushes the grass and dirt off Breanne as they watch the tail end of the massive bird flock speed away to who knows where.

"We better go find the kids and fast!" Breanne warns.

Ellis just nods, a look of growing concern creasing his face.

A growling two-meter wave roars over the lifeboat sending the girls sprawling. They're knocked from its relative safety of the boat into the murk of the dead.

The east coast expression, ' Ass over tit! ' seems an apt way to describe what happens to Jill and Claire when they smash through the surface of the water. Disoriented, waterlogged and freezing they clamber in the direction of the surface and when they break through they gasp and suck in the fetid, but life preserving air. The seas roil and crash all around them and Jill manages to point shoreward and begins to swim with determined ferocity. Claire soon follows and taps into her remaining energy stores, that are almost spent.

The jaws of the boys drop as they witness the capsizing of the lifeboat.

Jimmy speaks volumes when he sighs, "Oh, no!"

The black and pregnant clouds give birth to their offspring and baseball-sized hailstones crash down on the fleeing girls. The stones explode when they hit the dark water and draw blood where they come in contact with human flesh. And blood now streams down the pained faces of Claire and Jill as they have both been struck numerous times by the deadly stones. They tread water, glance at the far away shore and at the fast-receding seaward lifeboat that has capsized but remains afloat.

Claire cries, "I won't make it to shore!"

Jill nods, "Me neither! We need cover!"

Claire nods, "Let's go, I think I can make it that far."

The girls swim after the lifeboat which remains tantalizingly - just out of reach. They finally catch it and get underneath and away from the hail. The air pocket is dim and Jill can just make out her friend Claire's silhouette. Neither girl says a word as they catch their breath and enjoy the respite from the hail. The icy chunks pound the hull of the lifeboat, and the storm howls.

Jimmy and Eugene are so engrossed with keeping their eyes firmly fixed on the capsized lifeboat, they don't hear Ellis and Breanne come running up behind them.

Ellis, "Are you guys okay?"

The boys don't turn around but Jimmy replies, "Ya, fine."

Breanne questions them, "Where are the girls?"

Simultaneously, the boys point out to sea and pinpoint the overturned lifeboat and say, "In there!"

And at that precise moment, they all hear a blood-curdling scream that emanates from the lifeboat. The sound is terrifying and made even more horrific by the shape of the lifeboat which both muffles and reverberates the screams of Jill and Claire!

Jill's breathing has slowly returned to normal and she feels an unfamiliar wave of calm wash over her. As time has passed and her eyes have adjusted to the dim interior of the air pocket, she can now make out the features of her new friends face. A face she finds reassuring and which adds to her sense of calm. And for the first time in hours both girls smile.

Claire is about to say something like, "What an adventure? Or maybe the storm will blow over!"

But she doesn't get a chance. Her new friend Jill's face has begun to change. Her lovely smile is now morphing into an expression of dread and disbelief and her skin has gone pasty. And Jill isn't looking directly at her; she's looking behind her.

What's she looking at?

Claire whips her head around just in time to witness Annie's gaunt and grub-colored face break the surface of the water from below. Some of the flesh has been eaten away from the skull. Her eyes sit deep and way back in her eye sockets and her rotting teeth are set in a rictus grin that spreads even further when she smiles at the girls. Claire turns back to her new best friend, Jill, and simultaneously they scream at the top of their lungs.

Mr. and Mrs. Crowells, who thus far have been absent from the action, drowsily begin to wake up after a post coital nap. Even though their family history has been forgotten, they are still able to hone in on the best shagging sites on the island. It's been ages since they've ' gone at it ' and when their twins met the other twins they knew they had to make use of the gift of time alone. The reason they are rising from their satisfied slumber is the sound of one of their children screaming at the top of his or her lungs. All good parents have the ' sense ' and the Crowells are no exception.

Mr. Crowells, "Eugene?"

Mrs. Crowells, "Claire, I think."

Mr. Crowells, "Direction?"

Mrs. Crowells shrugs and scans three hundred and sixty degrees.

A black mass moves, at incredible speed, towards them and away from Blond Rock.

The naked couple rise to their feet and shield their eyes and squint trying to figure out what it is.

"Bats?"

"Sparrows? Don't they do that thing where they fly like a school of fish?"

"Jesus Christ!"

"What is it?"

"DIVE FOR COVER!"

And they do just that as the exodus, of all manner of sea bird, flees the messed up other dimensional horror world of Annie. Over the cacophony of beating wings and panicked birdcalls, the Crowells try and communicate but their voices are drowned out.

Mrs. Crowells, "Where are the kids?"

Mr. Crowells, "Blond Rock!"

Mrs. Crowells, "Why Blond Rock?"

Mr., Crowells, "That's where the birds came from!"

Mrs. Crowells nods and they quickly don their clothes and head for their children. All thoughts, of their breathtaking climax, sadly forgotten.

Eugene and Jimmy stand ankle deep in the frigid water and study the overturned lifeboat for any movement. The screams of their sisters chilled them to the bone and their muscles are constricted to the point of pain.

(What can they do?)

The feeling of helplessness overwhelms the boys so much that they can't talk or scream out on their own. And as if the situation wasn't bad enough, they don't even realize that they clasp each others hands – a major faux pas in the code of hunky guys! But they are scared shitless and perhaps the group of boys who decide such things will show leniency?

The Germans, even though burned to quite serious degrees, have not been idle.

(An idle German you might be exclaiming in disbelief to yourself!

Is there such a thing?)

(In the case of our bird watching Germans, the answer is no!)

A few of the men, drooling as they thought about a cold beer, were motivated to scour the island for any possible sign that there might be a bar or at least the dregs of someone's long lost bottle. And it wasn't just a few of the men – it was all of them. Sniffing around the island like a pack of chubby sun blistered two legged bloodhounds on the scent of a lager or perhaps some rum. After all, pirates drank rum and there had to be pirates on the island. Or British Seamen perhaps hiding a grog ration? Anyway, one of the blood-hounds stumbled upon the tromped down tall grasses where the Crowells ' went at it ' and which now resembles a Rorschach test crop-circle. Low and behold, he - the German bloodhound, finds a rather large bottle of Amaretto that has hardly been touched.

(No doubt the panty remover of choice of Mr. Crowells!)

Annie lowers her head, which makes her look even more horrifying and addresses Claire and Jill, "Come join me girls, I'm ever so lonely!"

Her voice is more of a hiss or the sound of someone speaking who had no vocal chords. Annie used to have vocal chords but they've long since rotted away and been nibbled on by the creatures of the sea. A bulbous and fleshy sea slug wriggles through the hole vacated by Annie's vocal chords, leaving a coating of thick slime.

Claire and Jill salivate in response to the disgusting spectacle, their stomachs heaving once more.

Jill tries to block out the sight of Annie's ghoulish face with one hand and she begins to sob, "Why can't you just go away and leave us alone, we don't want to be here or with you!"

Claire swims up beside Jill so her back won't be to Annie and to stick together -the living with the living.

"You summoned me! Stupid, silly girls." Annie hisses with delight, "We are going to be fast friends for ever and ever!"

Two other heads break the surface of the black water on either side of Annie.

A young woman, wearing a black lace funeral veil – a home for several white thin worms that crisscross through the algae encrusted lace and into the nose and eye sockets. She stares mournfully at the girls.

The other newcomer is a First Nations man, half of his face cleaved away by an axe, and his exposed brains resemble a mass of oyster flesh that oozes and drips out onto his yellow teeth.

The young woman, First Nations man and Annie smile at the girls and in unison promise, "For ever and ever!"

Ellis and Breanne, still standing on the dry beach, try and take it all in. Their son, Jimmy, who never shuts up, stands silently and pillar-like. He stands in the surf holding onto another boys hand and they both seem terrified. And they could have sworn they heard the muffled scream of their daughter coming from underneath the old over turned lifeboat floating far out in the sea.

Ellis breaks the silence, "Honey?"

Breanne turns toward the sound of her husband's voice, seemingly the only living thing on Seal Island. Ellis is kneeling in the sand and looking at something sitting in orderly fashion.

Pieces of something.

"What is it? What are you looking at?" Breanne inquires, hoping for an answer that might make some sense and any kind of sense would do, right now.

Ellis turns to face her, the blood draining from his face as she watches, "You better see this."

He gestures to the pieces of something. Breanne takes a deep and courageous breath and begins to slowly put one trembling foot in front of the other.

Mr. and Mrs. Crowells have made good time traversing the island and in minutes they feel the sand and pebbles under their bare feet as they survey the odd happenings of Blonde Rock. Another adult couple, the other set of twins parents, are on their hands and knees staring at glittering pieces of something on top of the sand. Their son, Eugene, stands, stock still, in the surf, holding hands with another boy and staring transfixed at an ancient over turned lifeboat floating far out from the shore. But what they don't see is any sign of the girls!

"Eugene! Where's Claire?" Mrs. Crowells demands of her young son.

Eugene doesn't reply but points to the lifeboat with his free hand.

Mr. Crowells takes a different approach and runs over to Ellis and Breanne, "Where are the girls?"

Ellis, his face ashen, turns to Mr. Crowells and sits down hard on his ass. He regards Mr. Crowells curiously then points to the lifeboat, "They're in there!"

Mr. and Mrs. Crowells, "WHAT?" and they both hold their head in their hands not knowing what to do next?

Do they swim out to the lifeboat and rescue their daughter?

Do they chastise the other couple for seemingly doing nothing?

How do they know the girls are under the lifeboat?

This majorly SUCKS!

Breanne, having had more time to digest the current information - no matter how bizarre it might sound, decides for them.

"You better come over here and take a look for yourself!" Breanne says flatly trying to sound sane.

Mr. and Mrs. Crowells look at one another and nod and zigzag their way over to the patch work mirror that the boys cobbled together earlier.

Mr. Crowells glances at the mirror shards skeptically and spits, "And just what the hell am I supposed to be looking at?"

Breanne, unperturbed by Mr. Crowells' spitting, patiently points to a group of shards near her left hand that reflect the dim black and white reflection of the girls under the lifeboat and their creepy guests.

And poor Mr. Crowells, who happens to teach science in high school and is firmly convinced we've been to the moon, looses any semblance of composure and scientific method and drops to his knees in surrender.

He looks up to the heavens where the God he doesn't believe in reigns and pleads, "Really?"

The football loving male Germans have made fast work of the Amaretto and seeing it's an unusually warm day – they pass out where they stand.

(One shudders to think about the brutality of their upcoming hangovers having consumed all that sweet liquor and scorched themselves in the sun.)

The German women, on the other hand, are non-plussed and have seen it all before. A few ' Dummkapf's ' are thrown around as the women collect their things.

They've noticed a commotion on the far beach and being German and so efficient, they've realized that their bird identification charts will not be completed so they may as well investigate.. So off they go to join the Crowells, Breanne and Ellis, Eugene and Jimmy while their husbands drool onto the warm ground on which they sleep.

Ellis rockets to his feet, rushes over to Mr. Crowells and holds him by the shoulders, "Can you swim? We've got to get the girls!"

Ellis's words have the desired affect and Mr. Crowells grabs Ellis' shoulders and exclaims. "Damn straight, let's go!"

The men stride into the surf determined to bring their daughters back to shore and kick some ghoul ass!

Their wives, in tears and feeling very unbalanced at the news and views of their children in such a gawd-awful alien world, huddle together over the makeshift mirror. They are so consumed with fear and future grief that they haven't noticed their gallant husbands marching off to battle.

The two men stride and slosh by their sons which breaks the two boys trance-like state and they too fly into action!

(But not the action you might expect.)

The boys, terrified at the thought of what their fathers are about to attempt, revert to a much younger age and behavior. *(Oh, say, two or three-year-olds.)* They race after their fathers and attach themselves to their father's legs making it very difficult for Ellis and Mr. Crowells to charge into the sea bravely! In fact, the boys are so heavy that the men have to stop and catch their breath.

"What the hell are you guys doing? " Ellis uncharacteristically demands of the boys.

Jimmy looks up at his father with pooling, pleading eyes, "Don't go out there Dad, you won't be able to see them!"

Mr. Crowells reacts first, "What do you mean?"

"The girls aren't under the boat in this dimension – you can't reach them!" Eugene answers.

"Ridiculous!" Mr. Crowells sings, "That's impossible."

Jimmy stands up tall. dripping with sea water, "It' s true, the only thing that can react in their dimension are things from that dimension or time!"

"Like the lifeboat!" Ellis adds. "Did you guys send the boat?"

Eugene jumps up and joins Jimmy and they both beam and nod their heads,

"Brilliant!" Ellis says proudly.

"This is bullshit!" Mr. Crowells says with incredulity, "What really happened? Where are your sisters?"

Unfazed. Jimmy and Eugene point to the lifeboat.

The German women arrive just as Mr. Crowells stubbornly begins to swim toward the lifeboat. They excitedly chat among themselves and wave at the departing Mr. Crowells. They also naturally assume that Mr. Crowells is off on a leisurely swim and that this is the best spot on Seal Island for watersports. The German women waste no time in dropping their drawers, so to speak, and contradicting the notion of European modesty.

The naked German ladies are an interesting sight and an example of contrasts. Their sagging, floppy and jiggling flesh for the most part is the color of lard or vegetable shortening. *(For all you vegans!)* But where their flesh was exposed to the sun, it's a color - any East Coast lobster would be proud of!

Jimmy and Eugene giggle behind their mouth-covering hands - thinking the sight, the funniest thing they have ever seen and perhaps the most gross as they have yet to appreciate the opposite sex.

Ellis has to steady himself with hands on knees as this new development in a very messed up scenario has taken a detour he never suspected.

Much better than chicken dancing Nazi's! he chuckles in his inside voice.

Breanne and Mrs. Crowells unconsciously cover themselves with their hands even though they are fully clothed. They are also unsure of what to say to their sons. They have always practiced acceptance and the celebration of the diversity of the world.

And that our bodies are nothing to be ashamed of. But now that they are faced with a naked group of German ladies – they have no idea how to proceed!

Breanne glances at Mrs. Crowells who just shrugs.

But their uncertainty and embarrassment is soon alleviated as the Germans splash into the surf and head in the direction of Mr. Crowells who is fast approaching the lifeboat.

Ellis, Breanne and Mrs. Crowells study the shards and they all gasp. Their wonderful, beautiful, innocent daughters are facing off with three hideous creatures. They look human but are so decayed and disgusting that everyone's imaginations are stretched to snapping. No prosthetic horror artist has ever imagined what they see in the broken and jagged bits of mirror!

Their hearts sink!

The Germans, now in deep water, watch Mr. Crowells slip under the side of the over turned lifeboat. This causes a bit of a stir as the naked German ladies discuss the merits and pitfalls of joining Mr. Crowells under said lifeboat.

The merits being:

Possibly being accidently or purposely felt up by a strange man as it's been years since any of the ladies have ' gone at it '!

The adventure of finding out what it's like under an over-turned lifeboat.

The possibility of drowning Mr. Crowells as an act of revenge against all men for being drunken, non-sexual, football loving bastards!

The pitfalls being:

Possibly being accidently or purposely felt up by a strange man as it's been years since any of the ladies have ' gone at it '!

Bugs and other vile creatures are probably competing with one another for survival in the air pocket under said lifeboat.

And in the end, the pitfalls win out!

The naked German ladies decide that the best place to practice floating on their backs is next to an inter-dimensional rift where horrid creatures threaten the lives of two young and sweet girls.

And that's just what they do.

Poor Ellis can hardly take it anymore as seemingly each moment near Blonde Rock becomes even more bizarre than the next. The site of the naked German ladies floating on their backs right next to the horrific - will stick with him for a long, long time!

Mr. Crowells adjusts to the dimness of the over-turned lifeboat and tries to catch his breath. He's been neglecting his normal fitness regimen of late and the swim has exhausted him.

"Well, that and giving my wife a good pounding!" he brags to himself.

"That stench! Jesus! "

Smells like a porta potty at the kids festival on a sunny day, he also thinks to himself.

As far as he can tell, in the dark air-pocket of the lifeboat, there's nothing that could cause such a rank odor and in fact there is nothing there at all.

No daughters!

He does however notice an abundance of insects and small creatures sharing the same air pocket.

(Those wily Germans! How did they know?)

In Annie's domain, there's been a change. An ever so subtle change in the air pressure or perhaps the light. Annie, the seeming queen of the ghouls, notices the change first and she regards the space right beside the girls with a grin.

"He can't help you!" she laughs.

Claire and Jill, purple from the cold water and shivering uncontrollably, study the space beside them but can't see anything.

"No one can help you. This is your new home and what fun we'll have.!" Annie promises.

The remaining gelatinous eye of the cleaved First Nations man, oozes out of the socket like a triple scoop vanilla ice cream cone on an August day. The eye hangs by the last still intact nerve and he looks from one girl to the other.

"Shall we go to the garden?" Annie entices.

 The g g g g garden?" Jill shivers.

The corpse, with the wormy veil, hisses, "It's wonderful."

"It will take your breath away!" Annie assures the girls will a sinister tone, "It's not far. Just down to the bottom."

"All the way down!" the woman with the veil and First Nation's man promise in unison.

Mr. Crowells swims slowly past the floating Germans on his way back to shore. He swims slowly as he's dog-tired and worries that he doesn't have the stamina to make it back.

The male part of his brain jauntily adds, "That's because you banged your wife and spectacularly!"

The German ladies decide to end their floating session and follow Mr. Crowells as he seems to know what he's doing. And the ladies who were hoping for some innocent fun under the lifeboat, can at least look at his bum!

On shore, Ellis, Breanne, Eugene, Jimmy and Mrs. Crowells study the mirror shards and try and hold in their panic and more importantly come up with a solution.

Mrs. Crowells, who was at first a bit skeptical about other dimensions and revolting animated corpses, is now fully on board. She watched her husband slip under the over turned lifeboat in real life but could not see him in Annie world.

And speaking of which, Mr. Crowells hauls himself out of the icy water and crawls on hands and knees onto the dry shore. He gasps for breath and is probably close to a heart attack.

No one makes a move to help him, being too engrossed in the freakish events playing out in a world devoid of life and light and colors.

In the meantime, the German ladies have arrived and they decide to assist Mr. Crowells who has collapsed in a heap but is still breathing. They manhandle him to his feet and heave his heavy body farther up on shore. They then prop him against a bleached-out driftwood log happily nestled in the sparse grasses and sand. The ladies laugh and tisk, tisk one another as errant hands and body parts may have accidently brushed up against Mr. Crowells!

Claire and Jill do their best to hug each other for warmth and hang on to the side of the over-turned lifeboat. Hypothermia is now a very real possibility and the girls muscles are beginning to cramp. And even with all the contortions, they never take their eyes off Annie and the two flanking specters.

"W-w-w-wwe want o go h-h-home!" Claire pleads.

"Oh dearest, you are home. We'll almost. Just let go of the boat and drift down into the welcoming abyss." Annie coos, "What could be easier?"

"S-s-screw you!" Jill spits.

"My lovely, lovely daughters. You are barely hanging on and so cold. So very cold. I will have you one way or another. Please don't fight it. Just a quick gulp and down we go." Annie smiles as the maggoty slug that squirmed down her windpipe wriggles up and fills her bony mouth.

Breanne, Mrs. Crowells, Eugene, Jimmy and Ellis sigh mournfully. Jill and Claire are exhausted and terrified and quite frozen. In the washed out other world they look ashen and near death.

Ellis hides his head in his hands and whispers, "What can we do?"

Jimmy and Eugene step away from the mirror shards and look longingly at the over- turned lifeboat – their eyes misting with new tears.

Mrs. Crowells begins to mewl and sob and tries to will herself into the other world to protect and console her daughter.

She reaches a shaking hand out and cries, "What can we do?"

Breanne, feeling hopeless and helpless and teetering on the edge of consciousness, puts her hand up in the air in surrender and asks, "What can we do?"

Annie makes a swallowing motion and the bloated slug slides down her throat.

"Time's up girls! The garden of unearthly delights awaits!" Annie promises.

Annie and her two dead minions close the gap between the horrified girls. The girls try and back up as far as they can and search for some kind of escape.

"It will all be over soon and it won't hurt a bit." she coos, "Oh, who am I kidding – it will hurt a lot!"

Annie cackles and reaches out her once delicate hands which now resemble grey talons with miniscule bits of flesh still attached here and there.

The Girls think about screaming but realize the futility of such an action.

Jill stops thrashing about and stares into space. Claire gives Jill's shoulder a nudge but Jill doesn't react.

"Jill?" Claire asks with intense concern, "Don't leave me!"

Claire continues to shake Jill.

"Looks like your friend has already checked out!" Annie gloats, "It's for the best really – her transition will be less traumatic"

"BACK OFF, BITCH!" Claire warns and surprises herself with her virginal use of expletives, "BACK OFF or I'll KILL YOU!"

"But, daughter, I'm already dead! Dead for years and years!" Annie laughs.

"What's wrong with your daughter?" Mrs. Crowells points into the mirror shards, "Why isn't she moving?"

Breanne and Ellis study the terror tableau and respond with expressions of dread as new tears fill their already blood-shot eyes.

"Is she dead?" Mrs. Crowells blurts out, unthinking.

Breanne doesn't hear her or pretends she doesn't as she focuses on the otherworld as though nothing else matters. Ellis' mouth hangs open as if he might speak or reply but no words are forthcoming. He turns to Mrs. Crowells employing her with his eyes to answer her own question.

Jimmy and Eugene, having waded out up to their knees, stare at the lifeboat and in unison whisper, "Not yet!"

Claire has failed in her attempt to stir Jill out of her fugue. In truth she has given up with no fight in her left to give. With one hand holding onto the boat and one hand lovingly resting on her new friend Jill's shoulder, Claire glares at Annie through a torrent of tears. Annie grins, sensing complete and total victory over these feisty young women She gently places her own grotesque hand the same way on Claire's shoulder. Claire doesn't even flinch.

"There, there my sweet brave girl. So many tears! Enough to fill another ocean," Annie sings in a lullaby voice, "I will kiss your tears away as you drift into the long night. Drift away forever."

The tone of Annie's voice has crept past her freezing flesh and ever so slightly warms Claire's heart.

Sleep sounds good about now. I'm so tired. Ever so tired and Annie will wake me up. Claire dreams, *She'll wake me with sweet kisses.*

Claire smiles a reassured smile as she closes the heavy lids of her waterlogged eyes and lets go of Jill and the overturned lifeboat.

"NO, NO, NO, NO, NO!" screams Mrs. Crowells as she watches Claire slip under the inky water.

Ellis cocks his head, still hoping for answers from Mrs. Crowells but not really sure what's happening anymore and which world is real or not.

All that Breanne can add is "Oh God!" and secretly inside she thinks, *Thank God it's not Jill!*

At least she thinks she thought that in her inside voice. She may have said it aloud but she doesn't care anymore. Mr. Crowells shows signs of life at the sound of his wife screaming. His band of German groupies helps him to his feet and guides him over the sand and pebbles to stand beside his wife. Mr. Crowells and the Germans look over Mrs. Crowells' shoulder and gasp. The German ladies look at one another, look down at the shards and look at one another once more.

In unison, they whisper, "Scheisse!"

Mr. Crowells falls to one knee and places a hand on his wife's shoulder, "Where's Claire?"

Annie is about to guide Claire down to the garden when Jill's voice stops her and she turns back to look at the girl she thought comatose.

"Annie." Jill says evenly, her eyes bright and gazing at her ghoulish captor.

"I thought you'd gone away." Annie says with surprise, "You two have been a real surprise. A surprise of a prize!"

Jill smiles back and gestures to Annie to come closer, with her free hand.

Annie regards Jill quizzically and with some trepidation but decides to risk it. She glides through the foul murk and positions herself directly in front of the feisty young girl.

Jill innocently asks, "Would you take my hand please? I'm so scared."

"Why of course child. I'm glad you've come round." Annie purrs.

Annie clasps Jill's hand and is shocked when Jill squeezes it vice-like! She was expecting something more gentle and tentative. Jill laughs and squeezes Annie's taloned-hand even harder holding Annie firmly in place.

With pent-up venom and hatred in her voice, Jill booms out, "Here Piggy, piggy, pig, pig, pig PIG!"

Annie's expression turns from smarmy confidence to despair and dread as she realizes, too late, she's been duped. She tries to whip her head around to see what's creating the disturbance in the dark water right behind her but Jill holds her fast and begins to laugh in earnest.

Bubbling up through the surface of the grey soupy ocean is the Pig Man. He rises out of the water and raises his razor sharp clever. Even though the air pocket under the over-turned lifeboat is gloomy, the clever manages to glint.

The Pig Man smiles like only a pig can and screams, "WREE, WREE, WREE!"

The clever arcs down, at lightning speed, and hacks off the top of Annie's head! Decaying grey matter and wriggling sea creatures splatter everywhere and coat the inside of the over turned lifeboat. The clever rises once more and Jill, sensing the opportunity in chaos, releases Annie's claw and sinks under the surface. Using only her sense of touch, Jill manages to find the lifeless Claire and swim under and away from the lifeboat.

On the tiny mirror shards organized on the sand, Mr. and Mrs. Crowells, Breanne, Ellis and the Germans watch with rapt attention as a maelstrom explodes under the over-turned lifeboat. A new unnatural creature has entered the fray and it looks like a human with a pig's head. The Pig Man has decapitated the decaying woman, who tormented Jill and Claire, and raises it's clever again and obliterates the remainder of her head.

And as the blade found it's mark – the image from the washed out dead world winks out of existence.

Everyone looks back and looks at one another for some kind of reassurance but find none. So, they all return their gaze to the shards that now just reflect their own faces and their immediate surroundings, just like a normal mirror.

"SOMETHING'S HAPPENING!"

A shout from the sea turns everyone's head in that direction. Jimmy and Eugene point excitedly at the over turned lifeboat no longer veiled in otherworldly haze and mist. It rocks too and fro as if something on the inside is desperately trying to get out.

Metal ' CLANG, CLANG, CLANGS ' ring out and some of the boards seem to be coming loose.

A few meters away from the boat, on the landward side, pops the head of Jill trying frantically to keep the unconscious Claire's head up and out of the water.

"HELP!" Claire gurgles and spits.

The girls are a long way from shore and everyone on the beach weighs their options in their own heads.

Ellis quickly calculates:

Mr. Crowells is too exhausted to be of any use.

The boys aren't strong enough.

The Germans can float.

Mrs. Crowells is an unknown.

Breanne is just an okay swimmer.

"Guess it's me then," Ellis says to himself and surges into the cold water.

And close behind are the German ladies. Ellis smiles even though the situation has become one of life and death. He nods to the Germans, happy for the help and they nod and smile back. They dive into the water and swim as fast as they can to assist Jill and Claire. Just as they reach the hypothermic girls, the lifeboat begins to explode from within in a shower of sawdust and splintering wood and what sounds like a pig squealing! The rescue team surrounds the girls as Jill gets pulled under by Claire's lifeless weight.

Ellis grabs Jill and buoys her up with one hand and shouts, "Just hold on, don't try to swim!"

Jill replies with a relieved nod and goes limp.

The German ladies buoy up the lifeless Claire and begin to swim as fast as they can toward the shore and the anxious Mr. and Mrs. Crowells, the boys and Breanne.

The Germans get there first and easily haul Claire up onto shore and turn her on her back.

Mrs. Crowells blubbering " thank you's " immediately gets to work trying to revive Claire and begins mouth to mouth.

The Germans give her space but soon take over recovery efforts when they see that no air is getting into Claire's water-filled lungs. One of the ladies begins to push on Claire's tiny chest with her meaty hand and soon seawater is pumping out the sides of Claire's blue mouth.

Ellis has finally made it back and Breanne and Jimmy guide Jill's unsteady limbs onto dry land. Without hesitation, Breanne strips naked and wraps her frigid daughter in her own dry clothes. She begins to rub warmth back into her daughter who can do nothing but shiver and grin occasionally. Jimmy hugs his heroic father and both men laugh and cry and look at their daughter and sister with grateful eyes.

The sound of Claire throwing up a swimming pool - sized volume of seawater makes everyone laugh.

With the exception of the German woman who she spit up on who gasps and says, "Scheisse!"

Claire rises to a sitting position, coughing and sputtering and obviously distressed at the sight of all the naked German ladies who surround her and look very confused.

And out on the sea, the turbulence has stopped.

All that remains are broken and smashed pieces of lifeboat and what looks like a tattered piece of black lace. Slowly the pieces begin to sink and make the long decent to the bottom where the horror and secrets of the sea should remain!

Where the horror and secrets of the sea should remain!

Where the horror and secrets of the sea should...

The End.

In a secluded and breathtakingly beautiful bay, anchored to the fierce cliff-face high above the ocean, hangs Aegir's Offering. Not an offering of food or incense, mind you, but a pub. But not just any pub. Not like the usual Canadian pub where various foodstuffs are tortured with hot oil and batter and paired with ice-cold beer served from filthy taps whose arteries are clogged from decades of neglect.

No, Aegir's Offering, is probably the most beautiful pub you have ever seen. Gorgeously hand-carved wood made from the hulls and masts of Viking longboats adorns the interior. Most tourists assume the ancient wood came from Home Depot or Lowes. Ornate silver and glass sconces, Viking booty from the New World, bathe and illuminate the luxuriant but tasteful sea-themed décor. The main room resembles a Viking long hall with cavernous ceilings and long wooden sharing tables.

For this is no place to go on a first date! This is a place to be boisterous and make new friends and occasionally a few enemies.

And here on tap, we find craft beer made in small batches with lots of love and care and ingredients sourced locally. Beer that has never rushed by on the rat-dropping encrusted assembly line of big beer producers! *(which sound like Polson's and Ledrats).* And if you happen to be a regular at certain regular times of the year, you might be able to coerce the staff to dip into the special selection and pour you an ' Old Shoggoth '.

There's always something odd in every pub, in every part of the world, and Aegir's Offering is no exception. One giant wall, of the main sharing room, is covered in photographs. Black and white photos, Polaroid's, color prints and even sepia shots from the 1800's that are so old they crumble when touched.

And no one! Absolutely no one touches the wall, or the photos, except the staff and today that happens to be Mister and Missus.

"And who have we got today, Missus?" Mister says as he picks up another shot glass to polish.

He looks at his forty-ish face in the highly glossed glass and marvels at his ruddy complexion and shameless good looks.

"Goin to be blocked today! Another raft of American tourists, no doubt wanting to ski in July!" replies Missus, she herself polishing glasses at the next table.

She is also in her forties and has that wild and innocent look of the faeries, Scandinavians and the Irish.

"Jaysus, but your probably right and they'll be carting around a camera and a jar of peanut-butter hoping to get a shot of a polar bear licking it off their children's faces!" Mister laughs, an easy unrehearsed laugh, and Missus can't help but accept the invitation to join in.

"They are a funny bunch! Most of them though, they're all right and ya can't chose where you're born. Poor things!" she reflects, "Imagine the brainwashing! Poor little beggers think they're a super power still! Oh, the gullibility! Support our troops. Noam was right, what the hell does that mean anyway? Mister?"

Mister peers into his glass, momentarily transformed into a fortune-tellers sphere.

He squints his eyes and screws up his face then shrugs, "I guess they'll be supporting turning relatively normal young men and women into blood-thirsty murdering automatons!"

Missus nods her head, "About right,"

She looks at the huge clock that sits high up on the wall of photographs; the hands bleached white like bones in the sun. And if you ever had opportunity to clean or fix the clock, at the end of a fifty-foot ladder, you would see that they are bones, human femurs in fact.

But no one, absolutely no one but Mister and Missus cleans the clock!

Missus stops what she's doing and gestures for Mister to do the same.

"They'll be here any minute, best get the ski wax out!" she chuckles.

Mister chuckles too and they put their arms around one another's shoulders and sachet to the door just as a fancy tour bus pulls up.

And for the most part, this busload of American tourists are quite lovely. They' re loud and boisterous to be sure but respectful as well and they seem to be enjoying their lunch at Aegir's Offering.

(Who doesn't like fresh caught seafood and craft beer in a gorgeous pub overlooking the bay and the ocean? Perhaps you would be tempted to say no one or only an idiot but you would be wrong.)

Today, it's two idiots and they stand out from the rest of the jovial patrons quite noticeably. Even their own bus mates can't stand them and therefore they sit all alone at the end of one of the huge Viking tables. They pick at their food and have hardly touched their pints and their faces seem to be locked in a scowl. And for the time being Mister and Missus decide to leave them to their negativity.

Meanwhile, the rest of the tourists are all-abuzz as their tour guide, a young good-looking woman named Sheila, is about to induct the lot of them into the Screech hall of fame. Mister and Missus are delighted to pass around the shots of rum and are giddy with anticipation and curiosity. Who will kiss the cod and become a Screecher and who might upchuck all that marvelous seafood?

With their last two shot glasses, Mister and Missus approach the outcasts to try and at least include them in the festivities. The man and woman look at their shots of screech as if someone, probably a someone with a beard and a turban, had just pissed in their glasses. Mister and Missus can't help but smirk at the spoiled sports distress.

"It's just some local rum. It's a tradition." offers Missus.

The man and woman remain stoic.

"Military are you? inquires Mister.

(How did he know that? You might be wondering.)

Well, though he wouldn't deny it, Mister is not a mind reader.

A lucky guess then?

(No.)

You see our two rather unpleasant American tourists are dressed, head to toe, in blue military fatigues and they've had their heads shaved recently.

(Yes - even the woman - who looks quite sexy in a young Sinead O'Connor or lesbian kind of way.)

But here at Aegir's Offering, there is no judgment.

The man glares at Mister, "Marines. What of it?"

Mister smiles "Support our troops!"

Before the man and woman can reply, a rather roly-poly woman with blue hair proudly screeches in accordance with tradition. And then, not so accordingly, regurgitates her oysters onto the next table with a very impressive projectile fount! In the way, of said fount, sits a visiting football team from a Welsh town-no one can pronounce.

Mister and Missus wink at one another, obviously enjoying the spectacle.

The man and woman shake their heads in disgust.

Missus tries her hand, "Surely brave soldiers, like you, aren't afraid of a little booze from Canada? Though I'm sure it's better than anything you've got in the States "

The woman corrects, "That' s United States of America and you call this polar bear piss, booze?"

As if on cue, the man and woman down their shots with lightening speed and slam the glasses on the tabletop.

Mister and Missus are impressed.

"Like my wife said, polar bear piss!" the man states stiffly.

Mister locks eyes with Missus, "Well, Missus, it seems we have two brave rotted soldiers on our hands and they seem to be able to handle their liquor."

Missus nods sarcastically, "Seems so b'y, seems so!"

Mister decides to probe the negative pair, "Just back from a tour or on your way again?"

"We're instructors at Black Water, we don't go on tour!" the man snaps.

"We're in the shit all the time!" the woman brags.

Missus rubs her hands together in delight, "Mercenaries! Best kind! That's a pride filled profession now isn't it Mister."

"Oh, too right my dear, killing for the highest bidder, why Missus I may tear up and start wailing the Star Spangled banner!" Mister replies getting very excited.

The man and the woman shoot to their feet, fists clenched and ready for action.

"How dare you joke about the armed forces you draft dodging peaceniks! We provide stability to unstable countries, we save lives!" the man roars as his face turn scarlet.

The woman touches his arm gently triggering him to relax. The boisterous Screechers and everyone else in the great hall have gone quiet, now interested in the escalating situation at the end of the table.

Missus whispers, "Invading profiteers!"

Mister laughs, "Oh, that's a fine description! I was leaning toward impotent cowboys."

Missus nods her head in approval.

Mister and Missus fill the mercs glasses again and then turn to the other tourists and hold up the screech bottle high and wave it around.

"Get on the go!" booms Missus.

The tourists hurriedly pound back another shot and forget about the verbal duel at the end of the table.

Mister turns back to the man and woman, "Get on the beer, we was only messing with ya!"

The man and the woman look at Mister and Missus uneasily but relax enough to shoot back more Screech.

"Come along now, we want to show you something that I think you'll find quite interesting." Missus encourages as she and Mister walk jauntily away and beckon.

Still uneasy, the man and woman follow along behind, at a training ground safe distance.

At the far corner of the great hall, far away from the now pissed tourists, Mister and Missus stand patiently next to the wall of photographs and wait for the man and the woman to join them.

"This is the military section of the great wall of Offerings." Missus reveals.

The man and woman study the wall, which is jammed with photos from present day back to the advent of the camera. And before the advent of the camera, there are quite a few painted portraits. The photographs and paintings depict men and woman of all nationalities dressed in the battle costume of their home country.

The man gasps, "There must be hundreds."

Mister adds, "Thousands!"

The woman, obviously impressed, looks quizzically at Missus, "Are they all war heroes, is this some kind of memorial?"

Mister and Missus smile in delight and in appreciation of the weight of the question.

"They certainly were brave souls and perhaps you could join their ranks?" Missus teases.

"You mean you think we should die and get our pictures taken?" the man asks.

"No, no, no." Mister assures, "We mean to join their exclusive club!"

The man and the woman regard one another with uncertainty.

Missus laughs, "If you thought Screech was polar bear piss, then we think you're ready for Aegir's Offering!"

"More than ready, Missus, more than ready!" Mister snorts.

"You mean the wall is covered in people who excelled at kissing a fish and keeping down some booze?" the woman questions.

"Oh no dear. It's a proper ceremony and it's been attempted for thousands of years but only the bravest and most worthy get the chance to join the club." Missus says luring them in.

Mister teases, "Well, Missus, we may, for the first time, have been wrong in our intuition. Perhaps these CFO mercenaries can talk the talk but can't walk the walk, so to speak."

"Too right my love. Perhaps they sit behind a desk sipping mineral water while they send young boys and girls to get their legs blown off in lands they have no business being in?" Missus dares.

"Blown to hell and back just so the country can accrue more debt and make the bankers happy!" Mister spits.

"Blown to hell and back so the Federal Reserve can print more greenbacks!" Missus spits.

The woman barks, "What the hell are you two going on about?"

"Where's this rot-gut your blabbing on about? What ever those pussies on that wall drank, we can down twice as many!" crows the man.

"Oohra!" the woman says and fist bumps her husband who says the same in that annoying way marines do.

Mister and Missus entertain one another with a look of mock exclamation.

"Oh Mister, looks like we was right all along!" Missus says reassuringly.

Mister smiles as he steadies his cellphone camera, "Now, let's get a nice shot for the wall!"

In a dank and dusty service corridor, Mister, Missus, the man and the woman stand at the head of a dark winding staircase. The man and woman try and peer down, through the darkness, and sniff the air which has become dense and salty. From a corroded ancient steel wall sconce, Mister heaves out a wooden torch and lights it with a whoosh! The man and woman flinch at the unexpected illumination then return to their evaluation of the descending staircase.

"Appears to be hewn from the natural cliff face but its very crude," observes the man.

Mister nods, "Good eye. It was carved with hand tools by Viking slaves a long, long time ago."

"The Vikings had slaves?" the woman asks.

"Everyone has slaves, my dear! It's just a matter of perception." Missus says with a grin.

Mister thrusts the torch into the stairway and gestures, "After you."

The man and the woman converse with their eyes and the woman demands, "We'll carry the torch!"

Mister and Missus smile and gesture for the man and woman to lead the way.

(And they do, proud brainwashed Americans that they are – not giving a tinkers cuss to well - documented horror movie advice.)

As they descend, the stench of the sea intensifies as does the temperature and the Americans take note.

The man remarks, "We must be quite deep by now, this better be some drink!"

Mister says curtly, "I assure you, it is!"

They continue to descend, Mister and Missus sure-footed from making the journey many, many times. The Americans slip and slide more and more frequently. The rough steps are now slick and mossy and the stench of decay cloying. The man and the woman continue their descent and after ten steps they stop and listen. The only sound is that of roiling water, their own breaths and the beating of their hearts.

"Hello?" the man queries, "Quit messing around!"

Mister's voice swirls around them, making it difficult for the man and the woman to detect his direction. The woman, for the first time puts her hand on the man's arm for reassurance.

Mister teases, "All is well, my apocalypse accelerating friends. However, you must go on by yourselves as Missus and I can go no farther."

"If you' re trying to scare us, you have failed miserably and lamely I might add." the woman boasts.

The sound, of the well-lubricated almost silent rubbing of heavy steel on rock, breaks the silence and then a quiet clang as if something heavy has settled into place,

"What the hell was that?" the man asks the gloom.

Missus laughs from somewhere in the darkness, "Don't be so shitbaked!. It's just a column of iron bars blocking your exit back up the stairs."

"What about you?" the woman wonders.

Mister laughs this time, "On the other side of the bars of course. Were gonna go home out of it!"

The sound of two sets of feet climbing the stairs grows fainter with each step.

"You can't leave us down here all alone, we're American citizens for God 's sake!" the man booms.

"We'll carpet bomb your backwoods country, you MOTHERFUCKING DEVIANT BASTARDS!" the woman screams with venom.

The footsteps stop with a crunch of leather on dusty stone.

In unison, Mister and Missus call back, "You won't be alone!"

And then they ascend again until their footsteps are no longer audible.

The man and the woman try and rattle the bars but they're locked into place and quite secure.

The man re-assures the woman, "Let's continue on. They're probably just messing with us and we'll eventually meet up with the bus group."

The woman, beautifully framed by the torchlight, smiles for the first time and nods.

At the bottom of the crude steps, they stop abruptly sensing a change in their surroundings rather than seeing it. The man and woman hug the wall and follow it around until they find another wall sconce. The sconce holds another torch that they light with the first torch. Illuminated before them is a large cavernous space and they spread out and explore as far as the light allows. More torches are lit until the man and woman gawk in awe at the immense cave that stretches out before them.

A sea cave with a huge pool of salt water that stretches from the crude rock platform, that they stand on, all the way out to the far reaches of the cave. A cave so immense, they can't even see the farthest edge.

"This is amazing! The sheer size. It must be three football fields to the far side." the woman gasps.

The man shuffles counterclockwise, eyes fixed on the upper regions of the cave. He slides to a stop when he scans the wall that reaches to the ceiling behind them.

"My God, would you look at that."

The woman tracks his gaze and her eyes bug out when she sees the ornate carvings that cover the sheer rock face. Giant Viking runes have been chiseled into the rock with intense detail. While the stairs were crude and functional, the runes are flowing lines of intricate beauty, a rock carving of incredible engineering and grace.

"Well worth the price of admission!" he jokes.

"Can you decipher it?" she asks, never taking her eyes off the pictograph wall.

The placid water begins to shiver, ever so slightly, as if from a disturbance deep within the center of the pool.

Due to the excellent acoustical properties of this subterranean amphitheater, the man and the woman hear a familiar voice that emanates from the middle of the cliff face some one hundred meters up,.

"Haven't figured it out yet?"

The man and woman quizzically look at one another then back up the cliff face.

"Mister?" the woman ponders.

"Right oh." Mister replies. "I have to apologize for Missus' absence but she was needed to help get your patriotic and very pissed country men and woman back on the bus. She sends her regards."

"The bus is leaving without us?" the man demands.

"Already gone my dear." Mister sighs.

The man and woman look at each other for the first time without their cocky American swagger. A swagger replaced by a look of fear and growing panic. They stand back to back in a defensive posture, eyes alert and scanning for any danger.

Unfortunately, they assumed that no one would be coming from the direction of the pool. Otherwise they would have seen that the water at the center was becoming more than just a little bit disturbed but down right agitated.

Mister asks again and with a kindly tone to his voice, "So, you haven't figured it out yet?"

The man looks up angrily, "What the hell are you talking about?"

Patiently Mister continues, "The runes on the rock face will answer your questions."

The woman screams, "SICK BASTARD! Is this one of your juvenile games?"

"Not at all, it's the truth. Now look at the runes and I'll help you with the translation." Mister encourages.

An unknown something, of truly massive proportions, is making its way to the surface at the center of the pool. The water is now bubbling and rising like a pot of water just come to a rigorous boil. But before whatever, this giant monstrously huge unknown something, breaks the surface to reveal itself - two enormous unknown something's drive toward the stone platform and the two Americans. Drive like torpedoes racing to their target just under the surface.

The man and woman study the rock face unaware that two sinister projectiles speed toward them.

"Do you see any landmarks that you recognize? This should be easy for two reconnoitering killers like you!" Mister jokes, "It might help if you back up as far away from the rock face as possible – the image may become clearer from distance."

The man holds his ground, stubbornly determined to figure it out on his own.

The woman, conversely, backs her way to the wet and slippery edge of the rocky platform and tries various eye-enhancing tricks to discover the mysteries of the runes.

"Wait, wait, I think I see something now," she says squinting and tilting her head, "It's the bay!"

"Well done by the Jaysus, you got it first try." Mister praises with a hint of surprise.

The unknown subsurface projectiles have reached the rocky platform. But instead of submarine torpedoes about to slam into their target, *(that we all secretly hoped would blow Mr. and Mrs. Black Water into a million unrecognizable bits)*, they just stop!

Their wake overtakes them and laps impotently against and up onto the rocky platform. Two little fleshy points surface like periscopes. They look toward the rocky platform and seem to be focused on the man and the woman. The one closest to the woman, who as you recall is practically teetering on the edge of the rocky platform, slowly begins to slither up the rock towards her army boot- clad feet.

The fleshy point reveals itself to be the tip of a rather large tentacle and its suckers propel it across the rocky surface. The other tentacle, focused on the man, remains in place not quite sure what to do with itself.

The woman dares the man, knowing how big his pride can be, "You've got to come back here to see it, It's the only way."

He motions for her to back off with one hand, "Ya, ya just give me a minute."

"You might want to listen to the Missus, there b'y! They's usually right." advises Mister from his lofty perch.

The man flips the bird skyward and at the same time stiffly and begrudgingly makes his way to the edge of the rocky platform.

The tentacle, assigned to the man, drops down underwater with a small plop.

The tentacle, assigned to the woman, who has almost coiled around her feet -whips back around and splashes back into the water. It makes a noticeable racket that the other tentacles will be talking about for months to come!

The woman looks down, at the water, with mild curiosity then returns her gaze to the runes.

"Do you see it now?" Mister patiently asks.

"Holy shit! It is the bay!" the man crows triumphantly.

"Thimble Tickle Bay in all its glory!" Mister adds proudly. "Though it's had many names and quite a few very hard to pronounce."

Tentacle one and two have resurfaced and wait patiently with just their tips protruding.

"Now look at the water in the bay." Mister coaxes encouragingly.

The man and the woman pour all of their sensory awareness into solving the runes. Heads are tilted; one eye is closed and blinked rapidly - all employed to the task.

Tentacle one and two, as if on cue or intelligently directed, pulse and pull their way on shore and begin to coil around the feet of the woman and the man.

The woman, obviously better at this than the man, hazards a response, "Are those tentacles, is it an octopus?"

Angrily, the man spits, "Octopus? Where the hell are you looking?"

The tentacles have coiled themselves as high as the man and the woman's waist just like a cobra might do. However, the coils don't touch the man or the woman and therefore, the man and woman, don't notice.

From high above, Mister says, "Jaysus but you're close! Not an octopus but Aegir hisself! Bless the Gods."

The man befuddled simply says, "What?"

The woman screws up her face.

"You might have heard of him. He's been called the Kraken but that's just so generic! Aegir blows his top when you use it in his presence." Mister confides in all seriousness.

"Oh, come on! A talking squid God?" the woman asks incredulously.

"Come on!" is the most the man can muster.

"I kid you not, ya child murdering robots!" Mister exclaims, "I can prove it."

"Well worth the price of admission," the man snarls and turns to his wife.

His face turns ashen when he sees her! He tries to speak but his vocal capabilities have failed him.

Tentacle one and tentacle two constrict simultaneously, holding the man and the woman fast. Like a giant blood pressure cuff, they begin not only to constrict but pulse as they do.

Blood returns to the man's face again, as it begins to bulge under the pressure. And the same happens to his pretty wife who is no longer pretty.

"By the old God's he is here! I told you so eh what?" Mister says with glee and reverence, "Blessed by Aegir you are and what an honor!"

The man and the woman are lifted off the rocky platform as the unknown giant reveals himself breaking the surface and hauling his bulk out of the water. He opens his huge maw, one hundred meters across, and roars his delight - the sound deafening and the stench of putrefaction rolls out into the cave.

The last thing the man and woman see, before their bulging-eyes pop like raw eggs, is the multitude of glittering cruel lamprey eel-like teeth. Teeth that sparkle in the torchlight like a cave rent from the finest crystal. Teeth to shred their flesh and pulverize their bones as Aegir, Viking God of the deep *(and Thimble Tickle Bay),* pulls them in.

Missus pushes a thumbtack into the top corners of a photograph of the man and the woman. She and Mister stand back to admire the new addition to the wall of fame.

Missus smiles as she nudges Mister, "Nothing more satisfying than satisfying your God!"

Mister chuckles, "He does like the crooked ones with the black hearts."

"So he does, so he does! None blacker than those two. Black water, Black hearts!" Missus says in a far-away voice.

Mister reaches out an arm and gives her a loving squeeze, "No time for reminiscing now Missus! We have another busload in a few minutes."

She turns and gives him a peck on the cheek and then they both smooth down their clothes and help each other look their best.

"More Americans, is it?" Missus asks.

"Bunch a nuns from Italy!" Mister grins.

"Jaysus B'y! Nuns?" she exclaims, "Oh, wouldn't he love that!"

The End

FRAGLE LITTLE THINGS

Where did you find him? her thoughts undulated into mine in five dimensions.

She probes my thoughts with tendrils like the tongue of a woodpecker wrapping around it's own brain. She doesn't speak or look at me but I sensed empathized motherly concern.

In the dancing flames, my firestorm memory burns into her awareness.

Not much to it.

No, a fragile little thing. A male I think.

Fingers outstretched, palms down, she redraws his shape in the ether, molding the molecules just above his body.

You will heal this creature?

My incredulousness disrupting and dispersing the surrogate energy body into a thousand points of light like fluttering cellular butterflies taking flight.

Are we not sworn to attend all the creatures of forest and the pure?

My gaze falls to the puny, mostly hairless abomination at my feet, still smoking. His blisters reflect the tongues of flame licking the cedars in the distance.

He is NOT of the forest.

She presses a long, coarse, leathery finger onto the blackened flesh between his eyes. Photons stream out of his closed eyes and construct three-dimensional images above his chest, rising and falling imperceptibly. Wave upon wave of stinking metal machines dump rot and decay onto the pure and still other machines drive it further into the forest. Wolves are nailed to posts by killers with projectile weapons. Salmon writhe in their own filth devoured by lice. She recoils as if stung, caressing and rubbing her finger. The images of callous destruction hiss out of existence.

He is not of the forest

I nod, satisfied in her realization, and prepare to end his suffering and wake him from his delusion. One blackened raw arm rises and searches the air, his wizened lips part. His hoarse faint plea is almost swallowed by the roar of the flames.

"Lost"
She looks at me quizzically.
What is lost?
The perfect description of his kind. A species unable to survive outside of their ugly shelters and without the use of instruments. When you first arrived in this purity, I gesture to the majesty of the mountains and grandeur of the rainforest, *Your word thought?*
She smiles, Home.
And his word?
Lost. she nods, *He is not of the forest. Before you release him let me look further, there is more*
My word thoughts, a wall of certainty, push her back.
There is no more. They shouldn't exist! A virus with hands!

The creature tries to sit up. She pushes him back down with one finger.
"My crew. Lost my crew!" he babbles.
Her finger hovers over his heart - like an osprey above a fish. Phantom flames surround us howling and hissing. A tempest whirls in myriad directions ever changing. More sickly creatures appear and rent and gouge the pure with long tools creating an earthen barrier to taunt the flames. The male creature throws his words into an instrument he holds in his hand.
"We're trapped! Cut off on all sides and the wind is sucking is into the firestorm! Ya. Ya. Are you crazy, WE'RE GOING TO DIE OUT HERE!"
He hurls the device into the flames and the other creatures stop and look at him, pleadingly.

"The bombers aren't coming! Neither are the heli…"

A giant cedar - glowing crimson, glowing white - explodes like an erupting volcano. The concussion lifts the male like a leaf in a hurricane and dashes him to the pure. The other creatures twist and scream as the heat remolds them into undefined shapes. She lifts her finger and holds it up. The phantom scene swirls away like smoke into the night sky. Her finger glows ember-like, marking the extinguishment of their lives.

Not of the forest, not lost. she raises her brow ridges.

My word thoughts swirl, a dust-devil touching down here and there.

What to do? I snort.

A multitude of hoof falls circle around us, settle and stop. A single doe approaches, staggering with exhaustion, her tongue black and dry and lolling from her mouth. So weak! We bolster her with empathy and calm.

I close my eyes and send gentle image thoughts.

Where are the bucks? Have they perished in the flames?

The distant reflections of fire dance on her beautiful brown eyes.

They were taken by those creatures! she gestures to the unconscious male with her snout. *They take the head and antlers and leave the rest to rot.*

"BLASHEMY!" I roar to the sky.

Everyone recoils. Even the flames recede for an instant.

She closes her eyes and bows her head. Her word thoughts cool my rage, Calm *yourself. This doe and her tribe seek council. We must hurry as the flames advance.*

The doe visualizes fleeing her burning lands. The sick. the old and the newborn dragged down by ropes of flame.

The doe sighs*, We are a tribe without land. Where can we graze and not throw off the balance?*

We close our eyes and bow our heads and the doe follows our lead. Our thoughts merge into image thoughts, three as one, and we rise above the trees and scan. A river snakes through the mountains to the south. Three as one, we descend and test the flow. Shallow and slow, an easy ford even for the depleted deer tribe. Three as one, we lift our heads and open our eyes. The doe sends an image thought of being harassed by bucks from another tribe. She caresses the doe's head and sends the image thought of the bucks giving way, respecting their plight. The doe nods her gratitude and the tribe shuffle away, their hoof falls quickly muffled by the inferno which inches closer.

These creatures, she gestures to the male, *They tried to arrest the flames, slow their progress.*

I stare at the helpless thing lying at my feet - unbelieving, *It appears so. How can this be? Has he awakened from the delusion that plagues his kind?*

She kneels beside him and leans forward with her hands outstretched as before.

I shall heal him.

So scorched and broken – surely he is beyond your skills?

I must try. He is not like the killers, the destroyers or the fire starters!

The cleansing fires bring life and diversity. Cleansing fire from a lightning-strike, wet and decaying foliage, all natural, all necessary. But the fire starters! How can the creatures let them live? We have no word thought to describe them. Abomination would be too kind.

She begins the healing cycle, his body flopping around like a grizzlies salmon, and I realize that his own kind have left him barely alive. Consuming and destroying the pure that provides them sustenance and shelter. No other species could even imagine such shame. The male stops flopping and she sits back weakly, eyes closed and still.

Would it not be a greater kindness to end his delusion? Surely, he'll demand it when he opens his eyes. And after all these centuries, my hands are sure and in an instant - release.

The male coughs and the river of life bubbles out of the corner of his scabby lips. He moans, agonized by his wounds.

Gently I whisper my word thoughts, *Will he live?*

He is beyond healing. The river of life spills inside his vessel.

Her eyes yawn open.

You will release him?

I will

The air becomes cloying as the heat from the fire encroaches.

I must be swift and sure as we have little time left to flee the consuming maw of flame.

Gently and with reverence, I place my hand over his face, swallowing his tiny head in my palm.

He slaps me away in panic and sits up screaming in misery.

The pain diminishes and he opens his eyes wide unable to comprehend the panorama before him. He stares at me and then at her and back and forth, terrified. His delusion, their delusion, does not allow for beings such as us.

Two as one, we caress his consciousness with tranquility and reassurance. He stutters and stammers, trying to speak, but the only thing that leaves his mouth is a spray of his river of life.

I tune my word thoughts to a lower frequency so he can understand; *There is no need to speak. No need to try and speak. Save your energy.*

He tilts his head as he stares at me like a wolf pup trying to free the meat from a turtle.

His singed brows furrow, "You can read my mind?"

She smiles, *Yes little one. There was a time long ago when you could as well.*

His eyes dart over to her, "You're female!"

She muses, *We have trouble telling you apart as well.*

His river of life drips from his nose and he wipes it off with his hand and studies it.

He gestures to his crimson stained hand, "What's happening to me?"

She sighs and swims into his eyes, *The flame of your existence diminishes, your injuries are beyond my skills.*

His eyes flash down his body, "I can't feel my legs!"

Tears roll down his face.

Do not waste your precious water on what cannot be undone! I gently scold, *The flames are upon us and you must decide.*

"DECIDE WHAT?" his words overwhelm us and we touch the pure with our hands to ground once again.

To be released from your delusion or roast in the flames like your, I review his word thoughts. *crew.*

He stammers, You mean euthanize me!

I look to her, brows furrowed, and she does the same. She gently touches her fingertips to his leg but he doesn't notice.

Your word thought is unfamiliar. Can you visualize the meaning? I touch his other leg, three as one.

This creature, as a juvenile, carefully lifts an old canine with grey fur up onto a shiny platform. The canine lies still and licks the creature's hand. Water flows from his eyes and he hugs and caresses the canine. An older creature inserts a device into the canine's forepaw and the canine yelps. The device is withdrawn; The older creature squeezes the juveniles shoulder and leaves. The old canine exhales one long lingering breath and is released.

Three as one we return. We remove our hands from the creature who shudders as more water falls from his eyes.

"You can do that to me?" he asks.

We do this for all creatures who need or desire it. It is our function, our purpose.

The inferno roars in displeasure - so close now that the skin of the trees begins to curl and peel. The cedar resin weeps down their faces in agony and burning memories.

Mesmerized by the flames, his eyes grow wider and wider still, "I don't want to burn."

She and I reach out with our hands, palms up.

I grin at him, *Do not be afraid, put you hand in mine.*

She sends him healing colors, *And mine.*

His hands are swallowed as we close ours. We close our eyes, three as one.

We take flight and rise high above our burning wards, three as one. We are of the forest, three as one.

The End.

PROSPECTING

A knock, knock, knocking on the door, to the rhythm of ' shave and a haircut '.

Ray rubs the sleep from his blood-shot eyes. Unfortunately it was only a half sleep.

You almost get to REM but never that deep - due to a snore or a puddle on your pillow. He props his eighty-kilo frame up on one elbow and rubs his six-o'clock-shadow that keeps reminding him to shave. He also rubs his armpit which reminds him that he stinks.

More of the same knocking but just a little bit irritated this time.

Ray, *(only his business associates call him Raymond)* sniffs his pits and grimaces.

He gets up on wobbly muscular legs and opens the door adorned with a small plaque that outlines the hotels rules. Blinding fluorescent light floods into his darkened room making him squint and shade his eyes with one arm-pitty hand. Leaning against the white balcony, of the upper floor gallery, is Sherie who laughs when she gives Raymond the once over.

"Holy shit, Dude! Been on a bender? Still on a bender?" she mocks.

Sherie, when she's not slouching, stands five-foot-five, weighs about sixty kilos and has shoulder-length green hair. She's moderately attractive, in a nerdy way, and wears big thick glasses to support the nerd persona. Sherie doesn't need glasses! But finds she can charge more when clients ask to ejaculate on them whilst still on her face. She prefers the term ejaculate and all it's variations rather than the term cum as Sherie has standards. In a pinch, splodge is acceptable.

Ray, on the other hand, is unlike Sherie. He has a conservative haircut, a muscular build, a hairy chest and most times is clean shaven. Respectable is the way most people describe Ray.

"What's with the green?" Raymond asks.

"Use it or lose it!" she exclaims, "Going to invite me in or what?"

Raymond waves her in, and scans the gallery before closing the door. He doesn't know any one here is Dawson City but old habits die-hard. Sherie plops down on the crumpled bed sheets and looks up at Raymond and studies him.

Feeling a bit like an amoeba under a microscope, Raymond asks, "Want a drink?"

She shakes her head from side to side, "I want you to take a shower!"

Raymond laughs, uncomfortably, but nods his head and does as he's told. And he actually feels better once the hot water sluices away the toxins that have built up the past two or was it three days? He's been waiting for the helicopter to fly him in to the survey site. First it was bad weather and then technical issues with the aircraft. Not that he minds as the company pays for everything. And yes, everything includes Sherie which he will itemize as a client meeting expense. He strides back into the room wearing only a towel. He finds Sherie, naked, on top of the unslept-in other bed - texting on her phone. Raymond notices her pierced nipple and belly button and pubic hair shaved into a slim vertical strip.

"No tattoos?" he asks.

She holds up a palm without looking at him, "Small talk is not included!"

Raymond shakes his head and snorts.

Sherie finishes her text and throws her phone onto the slept-in bed and takes her glasses off.

Raymond holds up a hand to stop her, "No, leave those on."

He drops the towel and stands next to Sherie and pulls her head forward.

The Downtown Saloon is awash in the din of a rowdy Friday night. Seating is at a premium which doesn't seem to be a problem. Many patrons have been here since mid afternoon, it's now nine pm, and they are so pissed they frequently fall out of their seats. Their ' so-called friends ' merely leave them stranded on the floor and take their seats with a small salute and not another look.

(The floor of the Downtown Saloon, by the way, could be eaten off of and other bars, in Saskatchewan for example, should take note!)

Raymond sits at the bar next to Sherie who has since wiped her glasses clean. They sip on bourbon and chat about life. Sherie has opened up and ponders her decision to leave her family and friends and make the trek to Dawson City. Perhaps there were more opportunities in Moose Jaw for a go-getter with a BA in the arts. She's still young after all, has yet to get the clap and is saving up to move to Gibson's. She intends to go back to school to get a degree in shamanism. Of course she has also heard that the Sunshine Coast is rife with the dark side and charlatans posing as guru's.

Raymond, you would think, would be fascinated with the musings of a nineteen-year-old girl with green hair. You would think he would be on the edge of his seat or offering to take her away from a life of ass peddling and make an honest woman out of her. Raymond is none of these and in fact is paying Sherie to be his date and is paying extra for small talk.

Raymond, counting the money this date is costing him in his head, blurts out, "I am so bored!"

Sherie reacts as if Raymond just dug up her entire family tree, doused it in petrol and lit it on fire. But being a pro, she quickly regains her composure.

"You should have said something sooner!" she exclaims.

Sherie turns away from Raymond and signals to the barman by sticking out her thumb and miming taking a drink. The barman nods and brings over a large jar of salt and a fresh shot-glass which he fills with more bourbon. Raymond, now interested, studies the jar of salt. He reaches over and picks it up for closer inspection.

"There 's something inside the salt." he observes.

Sherie and a few nearby patrons and the barman laugh. The curious face of Raymond is suddenly replaced by the horrified face of Raymond and he slams the jar down on the bar.

"What the hell?" he asks no one in particular.

Sherie giggles, "Time you were initiated into the sour toe club."

Raymond regards her quizzically and with some trepidation thrown in.

"Put the frostbitten toe in the shot and knock it back! You have to touch the toe with your lips or you have to do it again!" Sherie confides and demands.

Raymond snorts, thinking this is some joke being played on him. For confirmation, he looks around the bar and sees that all eyes are fixed on him. The eyes demand his compliance with good-natured humor but he knows failure or refusal would result in disgrace and perhaps even banishment from the Saloon.

Raymond, gaining courage, asks of Sherie, "You've done it?"

She grins, "You're the only one in here who hasn't!"

Raymond sighs; flips open the salt jar, wincing as he tosses the blackened toe into the bourbon. He tosses it back in one go. For good measure he rolls the toe around with his tongue in the empty glass before he slams it onto the bar. The entire bar shows their appreciation and his back gets slapped many times while Sherie squeezes his thigh and moves closer to his crotch.

Raymond sits naked on the bed with his back against the headboard sipping on a bourbon and watching Sherie. Naked at the bathroom sink, she wipes off her glasses with an off-white hotel hand towel.

"Want to spend the night," he asks.

She looks back at him via the cracked bathroom mirror above the sink and cocks her head.

"Really?" she asks, Most tricks want me out as fast as humanly possible."

"I'm serious. You've grown on me and tonight was a blast!" he muses.

She smiles too, "Okay."

"Is it going to cost me?" he asks with trepidation.

"No, you've grown on me too! And it's pretty late." she consents.

Ray listens for the sound of Sherie's deep and regular breathing and then grabs his cellphone and tiptoes to the bathroom. He quietly closes the door, before turning on the light. He opens a small compartment on his travel case and pulls out a small dark object. Ray grins, as he holds up his prize in the harsh unflattering fluorescent light - the desiccated frostbitten toe from the Saloon. Like Darwin might have studied a new butterfly species in the Galapagos, Ray scrutinizes the blackened relic delightedly. But his reverie is broken by the buzzing of his cellphone and he reluctantly swipes the call through then puts on a mask of welcome.

Ray mocks, "Well, hi honey, this is a surprise. How'd you know I was up?"

His wife's tinny voice replies, "I knew you couldn't sleep cuz you were thinking about me and the kids."

"Guilty as charged. How are you guys making out?" Ray smarmily asks.

"The kids miss you terribly and I'm so horny I'd rip your dick off if you came through the door right now!" she laughs.

Ray laughs too.

"Are you almost done? Are you coming home soon?" she asks hopefully.

"Far from it, honey. I've been grounded for days because of chopper problems. I haven't been to the site yet!"

"Oh Crap! What have you been doing to occupy your time, you must be bored. " she supposes.

"Ya, reading a lot and trying to take in the sights such as they are. It' s kind of a one horse town." Ray lies.

"I have a great idea! Let's have phone sex before we fall asleep!" she encourages.

"Ha, ha, I'm spent babe and I drank something that didn't agree with me so I'm afraid I wouldn't be any fun." Ray lies again.

"Oh. Okay then." his wife, disappointed

"I'll call as soon as the chopper is fixed and we're on our way. Love you." Ray lies one more time.

"Ya…" his wife hangs up.

Ray picks at his greasy breakfast. His eyes bleary with dark shadows underneath and his face still unshaven even though his hand has reminded him numerous times.

The restaurant is a buzz with excitement.

"Someone's cat must have had kittens!" Ray muses to himself.

The barman from the previous night spots him and stands beside Ray.

"Guess you kissed the toe just in a nick of time!' he marvels.

"Why's that?" is all Ray can muster.

"Someone stole it, that's why! What kind of a messed up individual steals a frost bitten toe that's one of the gems of Dawson City?" the barmen gets more agitated.

"Some sick bastard." Ray comments.

Before the barman can offer more gossip, he's distracted by some other Dawson City resident that is yet to hear the news. So he leaves Ray to his greasy slime.

A mop of blue hair plops down in the seat across from Ray. He looks up expecting to tell whomever it is to piss off but instead smiles when he sees the radiant face of Sherie.

"I thought only old ladies liked blue hair?" Ray jokes.

"Trying it out for future reference. Have you heard?" Sherie asks with some concern.

"Your cat had kittens?" Ray laughs.

Sherie looks at him quizzically, "No! The toe got stolen last night."

Ray nods, "I did hear. The barman is quite chatty this morning. You seem distressed?"

Sherie uncharacteristically fidgets and scans the room - perhaps the blackened toe is sticking out of someone's purse?

"It's the curse." she whispers.

"What curse?" Ray asks.

"Shh, keep your voice down." she warns.

Ray feigns acquiescence. Sherie is annoyed. Ray uses his fork to see how much grease he can squeeze out of his eggs.

Ray breaks the uncomfortable silence, "Okay tell me. What curse?"

Sherie excitedly leans in close; "The toe belonged to a prospector back in the 1800's. Seems he found a seam of gold and when word got out, the bandits paid him a visit en mass. Took the gold, all his tools – even his clothes. They left him out there to die of exposure and it would seem that he did. They never found the body but they did find that toe. His toe! And since then anyone whose been dumb enough to steal it ends up dead. And not just pass gently into the night dead. A horrible death!"

Sherie leans back obviously pleased with herself.

Ray leans back and chuckles, "Seriously?" he looks around, "This is part of the sour toe ceremony right? You all get another laugh at my expense."

Sherie regards Ray sourly, "As if?"

Ray laughs into his hands and Sherie gives him the stink eye.

She surges to her feet and as she storms away she spits, "Screw you."

Ray's laughter subsides as he watches her go.

He pushes away the remains of his breakfast and when the waitress comes to clear the table, Ray asks hopefully, "Too early to order a drink?"

Ray slowly comes to consciousness lured by the sound of rocks swirling around in water. He scans the dark room in a drunken haze but can't find the source. He props himself up on one elbow and looks out the front window which has the blinds pulled down to block the excessive light from the gallery. A man stands there is shadow making the motions of a prospector with a pan of water.

Ray cocks his head, "What the hell?"

Ray heaves himself to his feet, doesn't bother with clothes and swings the front door wide open. The man is not there but the carpet reveals a rather large water stain. Ray sniffs the air and bile surges to his throat but he manages to force it back down -where it belongs. He wrinkles his nose at the cloying stench of sour meat. He gags a little, shrugs and returns to his room and bed and passes out once more.

Ray paces his room with agitation, "Well, where the hell does the part have to come from?"

A few beats as he listens.

"Seattle? Oh for God's sake! So how long?" he sighs.

A few more beats as he listens.

"FIVE! Five days!" Ray hangs up and kicks the living shit out of the ancient and very uncomfortable hotel room chair.

When his fit has subsided, he snatches up his phone and wallet and heads out the door. Staring at him and grinning, a man dressed in eighteen hundreds garb, stands on the other landing across from Ray and nods. Ray startled, nods back and turns to lock his hotel room. When he turns back, the man has disappeared but even from the chasm between them Ray inhales the petrification and gags.

Ray spies Sherie in the Saloon but curses when he sees her arm is in another John's arm. She smiles slyly when she sees Ray. He dejectedly, heads to the bar and instead of sitting just stands and leans and orders a double bourbon.

Now what? he broods to himself.

He doesn't have to wait long before he becomes aware of another warm body standing closely beside him. Darla sidles up along side and bats her eyes, drunkenly. Darla has been around the block a few times and has the scars to prove it. Chipped front teeth, a few others missing and all a grizzled-yellow. Her hair has been dead for at least ten years and hangs in a tangled mess - partially concealing her pockmarked face. The layers of make-up would be more appropriate in a mortuary of which she looks destined and soon!

But instead of revulsion, Ray feels equal parts sorry for her – his save the cat moment – and with desire – his sleazeball moment!

Ray is a handsome fellow with a beautiful wife and has no trouble finding willing sex partners while he's on the road and even when his wife is out for a parent-teacher meeting. So why is he getting hard thinking about paying for sex with the prostitute swaying by his side?

It's his kink! His turn on! The thing his wife won't and can't give him. The skankier the better is Ray's motto! He only hooked up with Sherie because she was the only one left during a busy Dawson City business conference. Not that he complained though as Sherie was a kink of a different sort. Tonight it's all about this hooker on her way out and Ray can't wait to get his moneys worth. After more than a few rounds of drinks, Darla and Raymond negotiate a price and head back to his room where he does in fact get his money's worth and more.

Raymond wrinkles his nose as he marvels at the sour toe he holds up to the bathroom mirror. Beside him, Darla on her hands and knees empties the contents of her stomach into the toilet bowl. The contents include: her lunch, her dinner, the bourbon and Raymond's cum.

She must have had fish for dinner! Raymond muses to himself, *Sure smells like rancid fish.*

Darla heaves again, flushes, then sits back against the bathroom wall and looks up at Raymond.

"What's that?" she slurs.

Raymond shows off his frostbitten treasure, making Darla gasp.

"You're the one! Are you crazy? Don't you know about the curse?" Darla spits.

Raymond sets the toe on the sink edge and leans back against the wall, arms folded across his chest, ready for a good superstitious yarn.

"Curse?" he leads the witness.

"You are in for a world of hurt there handsome. Stealing that toe was a big mistake!" she warns.

"Why's that?" Raymond queries.

Darla holds her hand over her mouth, as she belches, just in case more than gas decides to make the ascent. "The owner of that toe is supposed to come looking for it and when he finds the thief, they usually end up in the loonie bin or dead!" she advises.

Raymond smiles, reaches down and helps her to her feet. He hands her a travel size bottle of mouthwash. Darla sighs and rinses several times, then leans in for a kiss.

Raymond pushes her away, "I don't want you when you're all sparkly clean!" he says matter of factly, "Time for you to punch out and head home." Raymond pushes her toward the door.

Darla pushes his hands off and collects her things, annoyed that she has to find a way home in the early hours of the morning.

In the open doorway she looks back, "Good luck, sugar! You're going to need it!"

And then she staggers out into the gallery corridor and slams the door behind her.

Ray stares at the closed door and laughs, scratches his balls, smells then and sighs, "Good times!"

Ray tries to focus on the glowing red numbers of the hotel alarm clock across the room. It waivers, in a haze, like a hot summers day and says 4:44 am. Same time as last time. Ray looks toward the door for the source of the noise – rocks or pebbles sluicing around in a pan of water. But the only thing near the door is the door and the harsh lights of the corridor blazing on the blinds. No specter! And still the noise persists. Ray is more annoyed than anything else at being awoken from his alcohol-fog - that most resembles sleep. He rolls his sweat-slick body over in the other direction and screams! Not a girly horror movie scream but a deep, trapped in a nightmare, scream that makes his neck-hair stand on end.

Sitting on the other bed is the man in the nineteenth century clothes. He's bent over his prospecting pan, swishing the pebbles around, and hoping some gold might wash out. He glances up at Ray and grins as if he has known Ray for a long, long time.

Ray modestly pulls the stained bed covers up to his chin and immediately wonders why he would do such a thing?

The Prospector's grin becomes a grimace of black festering flesh as he points toward the bathroom. Ray stares at him quizzically. The Prospector holds up his bare left foot. The foot is missing the big toe. The Prospector screams a silent scream and throws the pan and it's contents on Ray. Then the Prospector winks out of existence.

Ray wakes up with a start and glances at the clock which waves 9:00 am.

He smiles and sighs, "Only a dream", and flings off the sheets with a flurry.

Ray is in a better mood than he's been in weeks. But as he looks down at his naked, and once gym-hard, body he observes, to his horror, that he has pissed himself. Pissed himself, the sheets and the bed. And not only that but his cock, his beautiful cock, seems to be covered in crimson and black pimples!

After a scalding shower, Ray slouches in front of the bathroom mirror - dripping water onto the floor, uncaringly. He examines his body - starting at his head and moving downwards. His once lush and manly hair seems thinner and greasy even though he just shampooed it. The skin on his face seems waxen and jaundiced and tighter as if it shrank. Ray thinks he can see the veins pumping blood just beneath the surface. His eyes, now bloodshot and dim, have receded deeper into the sockets and thick black lines encircle them. The rest of his body appears to be relatively the same with the exception of his once beautiful cock. Not only are there many more pimples on and around his member but they've been joined by pustules. The pustules are sore to the touch and weep acrid fluid that has a noticeable green-tinge. He looks deeply into his own eyes and a tear begins to fall down his left cheek.

"Sherie?" he wonders then shakes his head no.

"Darla?" he tries to remember what transpired that night and closes his eyes to help the process.

In the blurry haze of Ray's memory, he revisits the evening Darla came back to his room and scans forward and backward like an old video editing deck.

He stops playback and zooms into the moment Darla, who by the way gave excellent head, pulled his beautiful cock from her halitosis dripping gob and asked, "got condoms?"

To which Raymond replied cavalierly, "Fuck that noise!"

Darla merely shrugged and reinserted Raymond's cock.

Ray's eyes snap open and he spits at his own image in the foggy mirror, "Idiot!" he hisses.

Dr. Selke, a young, well-built man, handsome, goatee and a red turtleneck, looks disdainfully at Ray, "Idiot!"

Ray's sallow-face turns scarlet.

"A man your age should know better! And known not to leave it untreated for a year!" the Doctor snaps.

Ray looks down at the floor knowing that this dressing down is long over due.

But wait a minute, did the Doctor just say a year!

"This just happened! It's only been about 36 hours!" Ray quips.

The Doctor stares at Ray incredulously.

Ray stands his ground.

"You're showing advanced stages of the clap, my friend, and you're lucky you're penis hasn't killed you. Now cut the crap! How long has it really been?" the Doctor folds his arms across his chest - daring Ray to lie.

Ray mocks the Doctors stance and with conviction declares, "I told you, and it just appeared! I'm not lying! Now can we get past this and decide on a course of treatment?"

The Doctor shakes his head in disgust, "Penicillin and tons of it! I think we should inject the first dose straight into your urethra!"

Ray winces, "To attack the source?"

The Doctor grins evilly, "Not at all. I think it's only fitting for a middle-aged man who got the clap and besides - I'd get a kick out of it."

The Doctor spins out of the room and yells down the hall, "NURSE! Get the giant syringe!".

Still feeling the agonizing prick in his prick from the sadistic Doctor, Ray drowns his sorrows at the Saloon. For the middle of the afternoon in Dawson City, the Saloon is unusually dead. Ray is the only one sitting at the bar and his mood is sullen. His first gulp of bourbon made him nauseous. But like any good alcoholic, he just waited for it to pass before he knocked back another mouthful. Ray glances at the salt container and notices that the toe he stole hasn't been replaced.

"No remorse from the thief I see. Do you think it will ever be returned?" Ray questions the Barman.

Mikel, a muscular and handsome immigrant from the Ivory Coast, looks up from his citrus carving; "They would be wise to do so before the terms of the curse have been fulfilled!"

Ray chuckles, "You believe in that mumbo jumbo?"

"The thief is a dead man! " replies the Barman assuredly.

"I wouldn't want to be in his place, that's for sure." he adds then returns to his citrus fruit and occasionally glances up at the football match playing silently on the television.

Ray mulls the information over as he marvels at the rust-colored bourbon in his glass. He alarmingly observes a tinge of crimson! He caresses his gums with the tips of his fingers and realizes his gums are bleeding. Upon further caressing, he find he can wiggle a tooth or two!

"What the hell?" he asks himself, then wipes the blood on his pants.

And while he does this he notices a wet spot on his crotch, an embarrassingly big wet spot!

Thank God the bar is quiet! Ray plots his course to the washroom and the least amount of alert eyes.

Once safely inside, he unzips and pulls down his pants to reveal that the entire front of his underwear is soaked. He slowly pulls them down, not really wanting to see his once beautiful cock again but curious to see the source of the soaking. From the blackening tip of his swollen penis flows a slow and oozing river of yellow and green pus! Ray careens back against a stall door which gives way sending him sprawling - but he manages to sit down hard on the toilet. He has left a slimy trail of said pus on the floor. With the burry eyes of an afternoon drunk, he follows the trail to it's original position. The Prospector stands there, arms folded like the Doctor and grins darkly at Ray.

The Prospector mouths the words, "Idiot!" then winks out of existence.

Hours later and extremely drunk, Ray tetters on a bar stool in the now crowded Saloon. It's standing room only and the crowd is boisterous and loud. Not unusual for places like Dawson City where the locals don't get out much and when they do, they give er! Ironically, there are two empty bar stools at the end of the bar that everyone seems to be avoiding. Some regulars, in fact, can be seen crossing themselves when they accidentally look longingly at the empty stools.

Ray's attention has been completely fixed on the bourbon in front of him and how the blood, from his bleeding gums, eddies with the subtle currents. Movement from his periphery makes Ray look in the direction of the two empty bar stools. But to Ray's surprise, he finds just one empty seat and the other one occupied by the Prospector - who sits much like Ray nursing a phantom drink. The Prospector senses Rays gaze and looks up and smiles through crocked and black teeth. He pats the empty seat beside him and points to Ray. Ray sneers at the man, from the century past, and returns to his drink. Occasionally, Ray glances over to see if the Prospector is still there and still studying Ray.

He is!

Sherie slams into Ray as she fights to the bar to get a drink. She's dressed completely in black and wears a black lace veil that covers one eye and one side of her face; She realizes that she has slammed into Ray who hasn't even noticed.

"Long time no see." she churps amicably.

Ray takes some time to focus his eyes and even longer to identify Sherie then slurs, "Hey".

"Jesus, Ray what happened? You look like shit!" she exclaims in horror.

Ray happily shrugs and smiles, "What's with all the black? Did the kittens die?"

Sherie grows somber, "You remember Darla? "

"Who could forget!" Ray snarls.

"She's dead! " Sherie says shortly.

"From what?" Ray asks, now very interested.

"Some std. Syphilis I think." Sherie says matter of factly.

Ray's face falls and the blood drains. He glances sidelong in the direction of the Prospector who pats the seat beside him again suggesting Ray join him.

"Have you seen a Doctor?" Sherie asks with genuine concern.

Ray looks at his drink, "Yes."

"And?" Sherie queries.

"Is there really a curse?" Ray asks tentatively.

"What? Curse?" Sherie asks stymied.

"If someone steals the toe?" Ray insists.

Sherie glares at Ray quizzically, "Tell me you didn't steal the sour toe!"

Ray uses the universal drunk language symbol for ' piss off '. This consists of him flicking something vile, but unseen, off his hand and producing a ' pffft ' sound. Ray returns to his bloody bourbon as Sherie shakes her head, corrals her drinks and returns to her mourning friends.

Ray snaps awake! An excruciating burning sensation emanates from his once beautiful penis. He knows he only has seconds to get to the toilet before he pisses himself. He tries to focus, his skeletal eyes, on the fastest route to get to the toilet.

But he can't focus! Not because he's had so much to drink that everything seems fuzzy. He just can't seem to make his eyes work.

"Focus, damn it!" Ray commands.

But he still can't see and the urge to piss is unbearable.

What was it the Doctor had said about late term syphilis? Ray tries to remember, *Was it jaundice? No, something that rhymes with jaundice though? Blindness?* "No, not...no, no, no, no. no. NO!" he screams.

"I'm fucking blind." he sobs quietly to himself.

Accompanying his sobbing is the sound of water being released under high pressure. But in this case, it's rancid urine, as Ray pisses himself yet again.

Instead of the relief of taking pressure off his bladder, Ray is in agony! It feels like all of his insides tried to exit by the same very small hole. Ray fears he will pass out at any second as his head spins and he begins to lose control of his muscles. But before he blacks out completely, a noise from the corridor jolts him wide-awake. The sound of the Prospector panning for gold.

"Okay, OKAY! Ya old bastard! I'll bring the toe back to the saloon." Ray acquiesces.

The panning doesn't stop but seems to be moving down the corridor away from Ray. Ray feels his way to the bathroom still unsteady from too much booze. He feels around for his shaving kit, finds it and digs for the toe.

He holds it up in triumph, "See, I still have it. Don't go and I'll give it back to you and then maybe you can find peace or go to heaven or whatever the hell happens when you die!"

The panning sound recedes even further and Ray tears out of the bathroom to where he thinks the doorway might be. But alas, it's the wall and he slams into it with stunning force. Ray slides down the wall, face pressed against it and pieces of Ray peel off and stick. When he hits the floor, Ray shakes it off determined to end his suffering by reuniting the body part to the man. He staggers to his feet and lurches out the door after the Prospector.

The temperature outside creeps below minus thirty-degrees Celsius and the time is 4.44 am. It's no wonder no one, in Dawson City, notices the surreal sight of a naked man covered in ugly weeping-sores careening down the street as if pursuing someone or something.

No one to gasp at the site or point or call 911.

No one to take a selfie with the hideous form of Ray in the background and post it n ' snapchat ' or ' pinterest '.

Like the mythical Pied Piper, the Prospector leads Ray down the abandoned street. He leads Ray to the outskirts of town and into the surrounding wilderness. He releases decades of pent-up frustration, resentment and anger by luring Ray into places even a sighted man would have trouble with. He laughs silently and heartily when Ray stumbles or trips or skewers himself on sharp branches.

Ray gets caught up in some loose rocks and goes down hard on the scree. His breath is knocked out of his shriveling lungs and he rolls around on the frozen ground gasping for breath. He finally catches it and lies on his back with his face to the night sky as if looking at the stars. Ray begins to sob uncontrollably, realizing there is only one outcome to his dire circumstance. He rages, screams and howls to the heavens, his last rally before giving into the cold and his body devouring STD.

The Prospector, annoyed at the delay in his cruel fun, pans his phantom gold with vigor - hoping to motivate Ray. But he soon realizes that his night of vengeful fun is at an end as Ray will soon be at an end. And with a shrug he winks out of existence leaving Ray on his own - far from help and fully exposed to the elements.

Ray clutches his stomach and groin, doubling over in pain! The white-hot poker of his urethra and bladder demanding to be depressurized once more. And poor pitiful Ray, beyond caring and embracing the warm embrace of unconsciousness and freezing to death, grabs his cock in readiness to pee.

His once beautiful cock, now fully blackened and putrefied feels foreign in his hand. A hand that has stroked it a thousand or even a million times. A hand that helped with the hardening just before penetration and a hand that wiped himself off when the deed was completed. But the flow won't begin so Ray gives his once beautiful cock a little jerk. But instead of encouraging his urine to flow, his frostbitten penis rips free from his body!

You might think that this act would be devastating to a man who regarded his penis in such high esteem.

Ray, now literally and figuratively numb from many such events, just snorts. He stretches out his legs and folds his arms over his chest and holds his penis like a body holds a flower in a coffin.

Ray imagines stretching out in a four-season sleeping bag right beside the fireplace in the cabin he and his wife built with their own hands. The place he loves most in all the world. The only place he has ever felt safe. He knows his wife must be close beside him and considers slipping into her sleeping bag and making sweaty love all night long. But he is just so cozy and drowsy all of a sudden. There's plenty of time to make love and all the other things on his bucket list. Just a little sleep and he'll be right as rain.

Right as rain.

The Downtown Hotel Saloon is throbbing with the rhythm of young voices chatting, screaming and singing, as it's the weekend of the Dawson City Rowing Regatta. The fans and rowers are packed into the pub like a sushi platter in a takeout container. Boisterous would be an understatement and the barman and manager have discussed the possibility of running out of booze more than once this evening. But even with this fire violation over-capacity crowd, two seats at the end of the bar remain unoccupied.

But that's true for some and not for others.

Anyone who has their head firmly inserted in their scientific asshole would certainly confirm, in fact, that no one, absolutely no one was using those seats. If, however, you believe in magic, the esoteric and that nothing is impossible then you might just see two men in those seats having a drink and enjoying the party unfolding in front of them.

Ray and the Prospector sit at the end of the bar nursing bourbon and smiling at the antics of the pleasantly pissed bar.

A young handsome male rower in a black muscle tee shirt sits a few chairs away - right in the middle of the bar stools. A young nubile blond woman who by all standards is quite hammered is flirting with him.

She sloshes her drink as she points to the white Chinese characters on the front of the rowers shirt, "What's that mean?"

He just smiles broadly at her - knowing that the characters really mean ' Zen ' and laughs, "It means Give er!"

She smiles and rests an adventurous hand on his thigh and says, "Cool."

The Prospector nudges Ray amicably and points to the barman who has just opened the salt container and placed it on the bar. The crowd hoots and hollers and dares the hammered girl to initiate into the sour toe fraternity.

The rower and the girl look at the salt, and then at each other, and at the same time yell, "I DARE YOU!".

They both laugh and reach into the salt and immerse their prizes in a shot of tequila and shoot them down with lightening speed. The rower laughs and holds up his empty shot glass with the Prospectors sour toe sitting lifeless on the bottom.

Everyone cheers.

The girl is not so gifted and chokes a few times before she can empty her glass. She regains her composure, such that it is, and holds up her drained glass with Ray's penis sitting limply on the bottom.

Silence.

The girl looks forlorn for a few beats then smiles and innocently says, "Looks like I choked on some guys cock!"

The crowd goes wild!

At the end of the bar Ray and the Prospector clink their ghostly glasses and smile.

The End

THE RECRUIT

"Someone I know, in the neighboring county, heard her one night." she says dreamily between small sips of Irish whisky, "Heard her keening just outside the window. Gave her an awful fright! The sound of her wailing, so hard to describe – like a wolf, snared-rabbit and a woman all screaming at the same time! But she remembered a folk tale her Nan told her when she was just a wee child. Her Nan said that sometimes all she wanted was to comb her hair."

Brushing away her own rusty hair out of her eyes, she continued, "and that's just what she did. She took the comb without a word and began to comb out her red locks as she drifted away. And my friend never heard her keening again."

Kilometers upon kilometers of sameness as far as the eye can see. Squares upon more squares and maybe a rectangle thrown in - a momentary loss of self-control.

The never-ending straight lined lazy architecture of suburbia.

This particular cluster of squares has been dubbed Scarberia, but not by the locals.

In this treeless cul de sac, something is just a little out of the ordinary. Instead of tattered maple leafs swaying in the wind from sun-baked plastic gutters; we see crisp immaculate Scottish flags not daring to droop in the summers heat. This enclave of Scarberian's are Scottish immigrants and you know what it is if it isn't Scottish! So proud of their heritage that they immigrated to Canada to bitch about how great Scotland is and how Canada sucks! Aye, laddie! It's Crap!

Pale and freckled bare feet caress the lush green grass. Grass barely a centimeter taller than the neighboring bowling greens. The delicate dancers feet gently make their way to a ' For Sale ' sign driven into the earth. The feet belong to Ailish, a beautiful, middle-aged red haired lithe Celtic beauty in dark gypsy - like clothes. She grips the sign with one thin hand and extracts it from the ground like a toothpick out of butter. With a flick of her pale wrist, jangling with silver and gold bangles, she heaves the sign over her house and it thuds when it hits the ground in her backyard. Ailish sighs, spreads her arms to welcome the sun, closes her eyes and pulls at the grass with her toes like a cat kneading a belly.

Her reverie is short-lived as the rumbling of an SUV pulls up to the curb, idles and the window whirs down.

"Just moved in?" a Scottish water buffalo bellows from the car.

Ailish reluctantly opens her eyes and squints at the sun reflecting off the blue SUV. Wedged, behind the steering wheel, is Jock, a real fat bastard in a Scottish football replica jersey that's at least two sizes too small!

Ailish tries a smile, thinking that this slack-jowled pudding in a car must be the welcoming committee and that invitations to barbeques and whisky-tasting will soon ensue.

So she calms herself with a breath and replies with a lilting tone, "Yes, just moved in."

"Then cut the grass, it's a disgrace!" Jock chastises as the window whirs up and he speeds away.

Ailish sways in place, a wee but stunned by Jock's unprovoked attack on her scandalously long vegetation. She recovers, takes another deep breath and holds her hand palm down to the ground and makes a gentle pushing motion. The grass, obligingly, recedes into the earth by two centimeters, making it the envy of the neighboring lots. Ailish smiles and makes a sweeping gesture with the same hand. She turns and strides into the house as all the grass in the cul de sac, except hers, turns yellow and brown.

Ailish, now eight, sits cross-legged on the lawn and sketches. She wears a black gypsy-like peasant dress and sits under a black parasol to protect her pasty white skin and freckles, her fiery hair in a single braid at the back.

The subject of her sketching is a very large brown-furred rat. The rat sits straight up on his hind legs and poses patiently by her bare feet.

Sean, a gangly boy of roughly the same age and not dressed in any Scottish colors, studies Ailish from a safe distance curbside, hoping for an invitation.

Ailish laughs, "Come over, he won't bite!"

Sean shuffles over to Ailish, not taking his eyes off the rat.

"Is that your pet?"

Ailish spits, "God no! Do I look like a punk from the eighties?"

Sean looks at her quizzically, "Huh?"

"Never mind. It's okay if you're scared."

Sean puffs up, "I'm not scared!"

He strides over and sits down next to Ailish. The rat follows Sean's movements with his beady black eyes but doesn't move from his art model posing!

(A real pro!)

Ailish smiles and nods to the rat, "Thank you for showing restraint Mr. Rat. I know Sean looks very bitable!"

The rat chitters back to her making her laugh.

Sean sits back incredulously, "He understands you?"

Ailish frowns as she sketches, "You've never swapped tales with a rat?"

Sean studies Ailish's sketch, "Wow, you're amazing!"

"Thanks, decades of practice!"

A border-collie puppy bounds up onto the lawn, body wagging with joy and curiosity. The puppy leaps playfully toward the rat - intent on play. The rat hisses in warning exposing it's formidable teeth. The puppy rears back whining which delights Ailish and she giggles and slaps her own knee.

The dogs owner, Magda, a pudgy teenage girl in blue shorts and a tee and flip flops, calls the puppy away and it bounds away toward her, rat already forgotten.

Ailish and Sean turn toward one another and simultaneously say, "Not long to live!"

Ailish, now seventy-five, sits on the steps in front of the house *(she's squatting in)*, further refining the sketch of the rat. She's barefoot and dressed in a black peasant dress. Her red and grey hair flows loosely over her shoulders. She takes sips from a delicate and ornate teacup.

Magda trudges along the curb, her body drooping and eyes downcast.

Ailish calls out, "Where's your puppy, Magda?"

Magda looks up and over questioningly, "How do you know my name?"

"Ahhh, Sean must have told me."

"Oh." Magda sighs, "Dad said he went to heaven."

Tears bubble just beneath the surface of Magda's eyes.

Ailish smiles, "That's good! Then your Daddy will have someone to play with."

Magda regards Ailish quizzically, "My Dad's not in heaven!"

She frowns, sensing a wrongness but only in a general undefined sense. Magda hurries away never taking her eyes off Ailish.

Ailish chuckles and returns to the sketch, "He will be tomorrow!"

Ailish, now middle-aged, relaxes on the porch steps, sipping single-malt and watches the sun set bleed.

Jock penguins up the sidewalk, sweating profusely with the exertion, and he frequently mops his face with a meaty paw. He stops in front of Ailish and bends over to catch his breath.

"Are you the one that's putting all the nonsense about dying in my Magda's head?" Jock snorts.

Ailish cocks her head, "Surely a teenaged girl doesn't need my help."

Jock snarls, "You sound Irish and a tinker at that."

Ailish smiles, "Ireland was the cradle of civilization where music, magic and the laws of living harmoniously in nature were born. What did Scotland give the world?" she holds up her glass and nods, "and deep fried Mars bars?"

Ailish takes a delicious sip then puts the glass down. From beneath her dress, she pulls out an ornate silver pendant, decorated in Celtic knot work and runes. She holds it up to Jock. Jock is mesmerized and his gaze is sucked into the swirling vortex of the pendant.

When Ailish speaks, her voice comes from far away and from another time, "Did you hear me singing last night?"

"Yes."

"I will sing again tonight and you will come to me and with me!"

"Yes."

"Make sure your affairs are in order and leave everything to Magda."

"Yes"

"Now, when you come to your senses, all that you will remember is that we had an argument and you told me what was what!"

Ailish hides the pendant under her dress and Jock holds up a sausage-like digit and fiercely wags it at Ailish.

"Got it!"

Ailish bats her eyes, "Got it."

Jock nods his whole body, waddles around and penguins down the sidewalk satisfied and feeling proud of himself.

A nearby neighbor waves to Jock who looks at her lawn and yells, "PUT SOME WATER ON THAT LAWN! IT'S A DISGRACE!"

Sean timidly inches toward Ailish.

Middle-aged Ailish grins, "Hello Sean."

Sean looks at her quizzically. "Is Ailish here?"

"Yes she is."

"Could you fetch her for me?"

"I could. Just a minute."

Ailish swishes and sways into the house, her bangles jangling. A moment later Ailish, now eight, skips out the front door with her sketchbook in hand. She smiles and sits in the same spot middle-aged Ailish sat.

Ailish pats the step and says, "Well, sit your arse down."

Sean giggles and complies. They watch an ambulance slowly drive by and Ailish enthusiastically waves to the driver.

"There goes Sheila!"

Ailish takes a sip of whisky and salutes the ambulance, "Off ya go then."

She turns to Sean, "Did you know her?"

Sean shrugs, "Not very well. When she had a few drinks she was a right bitch!"

Ailish laughs and shows her rat sketch to Sean.

Sean whistles, "That's incredible! It's so detailed."

Ailish rips the sketch out of her sketch book and hands it to Sean, "It's for you."

Sean, "Really?"

Ailish, "Ya, no big deal."

They sit in comfortable silence for a few minutes until Ailish belches. They both laugh.

Sean wrinkles his nose, "Your breath smells like booze!".

Ailish shrugs, "I'm Irish."

Sean studies Ailish then nonchalantly remarks, "Sure has been a lot of death around here lately."

Ailish gazes dreamily into the sky, "There is no life without death."

Sean grows brazen, "My ma and her friends said it all started when you and your family moved in."

Ailish glares at Sean, "Quite a coincidence! Maybe we're witches."

Sean, "Witches?"

Ailish playfully punches Sean's shoulder, "Anyone whose not Scottish must be a witch, right?"

Sean, "Is that called sarcasm?"

Ailish smiles, "I like you kid!"

They sit in comfortable silence for a few minutes.

Ailish studies Sean, "Can you sing?"

Sean shrugs, "Ya, I guess so."

Ailish, "And are you happy here, living here in Scarberia?"

Sean, "Where else would I live?"

Ailish, "Well anywhere! Anywhere in the whole wide world. Or everywhere"

Sean "Sure. Why do you ask?"

Ailish, "You'll grow into a handsome man."

Sean stands up, "I should go."

Ailish, "Meet me in the backyard after dark."

Sean, "How come?"

Ailish grins "Adventure."

Sean smiles shyly, "Okay." and runs all the way home.

In the darkness, Ailish takes Sean's hand and guides him along.

Sean, "Where are we going, I can't see a thing."

Ailish, "Patience. I promise that this will be something you've never seen before."

They stop at the outer-edge of the light cast by a large second floor window of a neighboring house. Inside, Jock, in baggy blue boxer shorts, sachets around the room with a large glass of scotch in his pudgy hand. He sings along to a traditional Scottish song ' Lochaber no more ' and every now and then he falters as the song brings tears to his eyes.

Sean laughs so hard, tears stream down his face and Ailish smirks.

Ailish, "Get a hold of yourself wee man. Believe it or not, that's not the funniest thing I've ever seen when I'm working."

Sean catches his breath, "Working?"

Ailish, "Move deeper into the shadows, watch, listen and learn."

She takes a deep breath and begins to sing an otherworldly ' Call to the Dead '

Come to me,

Come to me, now

Come to me now before the ravens take your eyes.

Before the flies lay host and the worms feast.

Come to me now before the wild dogs rip at you.

Before the molds wrap you in soft blankets.

Come to me.

Come to me, now.

Jock abruptly stops! He stands stock-still with the exception of his abundant blubber which slowly ripples to a stop. As soon as the song ends, Jock penguins over to the window and peers out but Ailish and Sean are well hidden.

Ailish begins to dissolve into black smoke which rearranges itself into middle-aged Ailish. As soon as she's completely formed, she sings a single high-frequency note that never falters and causes Jock to wince in pain and his scotch glass shatters into a million pieces. Jock staggers, sweating profusely, and his skin takes on a death-like pallor.

Ailish dissolves once more and reconstitutes into the shape of elder Ailish. She settles into her new form with a witchy grin and turns to wink at Sean, Sean stares back, horrified, the blood drained from his face like Jock's. She rises up on her bare toes keening and screeching a horrid cacophony of layered sounds that would curdle the blood of the bravest warrior. She glides into the light, cast by the window, and stares up at Jock with lightless eyes.

Jock sees her!

His eyes dilate as he clutches his throat and heart. Dark rivulets of piss stain and soak into his baggy boxers, a giant blue diaper. Ailish stops screeching and smiles beatifically at Jock. Jock's eyes roll up into his head and he falls backward like a thousand-year-old cedar and crashes onto the floorboards which audibly creek and snap. He's dead and stone cold before he hits the floor and his body turns from alabaster to robins egg blue. Ailish spins like a lithe dancer, arms outstretched and she morphs into her middle-aged form and then on to her eight-year-old persona.

Sean cowers and trembles in the darkness.

Ailish, "All done! C'mon Sean, don't be a scardy cat. Tell me that's not the coolest thing you have ever seen?"

Sean manages to stand on shaky legs, looking sheepishly at Ailish.

Ailish wrinkles her nose, "You pissed yourself too?".

Sean glances down at his soiled pants and back up at Ailish, tears brimming in his fawn like eyes.

Ailish laughs, "Sorry! I should have warned you that there's an impact zone. Don't worry. I don't care and what's a few dribbles between friends."

Sean smiles and straightens up. "How did you do that? Did you kill him?"

Ailish, "No. It was his time. Think of me more as a universal time keeper and collector of souls."

Sean, "Can anyone do it?"

Ailish, "No, we're a small intimate group and we're born to it. It's our destiny."

Sean sounding disappointed, "Oh, ya of course"

Ailish punches him in the arm, "Just like it's your destiny! I never bring an audience when I work, only recruits."

Sean's eyes widen hopefully.

Ailish, "Traditionally, it's just been women but feck me, there's seven billion people now and we just can't keep up!"

Sean looks at her dumbfounded, "You want me to do that?"

Ailish, "You're a natural! How did you know that puppy was going to die?"

Sean, "Oh!"

Ailish, "The first hundred years are the toughest and you don't get your other forms until you've actually reached that age! But after that you get to choose what form you take. I can't wait to see you at twenty-one!"

Sean, "Twenty one?"

Ailish laughs, "Never mind that now. Just think of all the adventures we'll have and I can teach you to draw."

Sean regards Ailish seriously, 'But it's not all fun is it?"

Ailish sighs and ponders for a moment.

"No it's not. But the times you get to harvest fat bastards like Jock makes up for all the sad ones."

Ailish dusts herself off and smoothes out her red hair, "Do I look okay?"

Sean laughs, "Your hairs a mess! Looks like a rats nest."

Ailish becomes uncharacteristically self-conscious, "Do you have a comb?"

"No, sorry."

"Hmmm…"

The End.

MENAGERIE

"Why if my Winslow were alive today, he'd knock your teeth out faster than you could finish your last sentence! Which is all BULL ANYWAY!" Betheny spits with venom at, her no good eldest son, Postal.

Postal isn't his real name of course. His proper name is Lester but his ailing mother claims that, walk-on-water Winslow - her dead husband, couldn't possibly be his father so it must have been the postman.

Like almost everything his mother says these days, Lester ignores the jibe.

Betheny gives him the once over and clucks at his fancy big city clothes – especially his brown sport jacket and shinny brown dress shoes. His toupee looks ridiculous and the color doesn't even match what's left of his thin greasy hair. Too skinny, with an overly large Adam's apple, and a potbelly or what is it they call it these days?

Shitbelly?

One of the trashy magazines, they subscribe to in this prison for senior citizens, had an article that claimed when they autopsied Elvis, he had over fifty pounds of shit in his intestinal tract! Thankfully, Postal's is only about twenty pounds by the look of it. God but he's an ugly bastard! Looks like a weasel. An old weasel with a twenty-pound shitbelly!

Lester notices the grin spreading across his mothers sagging, liver-spotted, wrinkled grey face and wonders what the wizened source of his inheritance is thinking about? Then again she probably just short-circuited another brain pathway and thinks she's the Queen. A thought which brings a grin to his own face. Poor old bat, confined to a wheelchair and all her friends passed away and those hideous production line Big Box clothes!

Must be the same sweat - shop that makes drapes, Lester muses.

One of the nurses lumbers by and comments on his mother's full head of ivory hair.

She's in her nineties and her hair is still growing like an eighteen-year-old!

Betheny calls after the nurse, "What kind of a son forces his own mother into a hell-hole like THIS! A WEASAL that's who! A weasaly mistake from a casual fling! And now I pay the price. GET ME THE HELL OUT OF HERE!"

The nurse stops in her tracks and spins, scolding Betheny with her finger, "Now, Betheny, you settle down! You know what happens when you get all riled up like that! I'll give you a sedative if you don't behave!"

"Just try it FAT ASS!" Betheny dares as she clenches here arthritic gnarled hands into fists, "I've never knocked a hippo out but there's a first time for everything!"

"Mother!" Lester admonishes outwardly but inwardly cheers his mother on.

Thankfully, KID has just clocked in and he gives Betheny a big smile. KID is an orderly. A giant of a man with a colorful Rasta hat. He makes music for iPhone games in his spare time to help make ends meet. He towers over Betheny like a giant amusement park prize teddy bear come to life. Betheny's demeanor changes immediately and she chuckles along with him conspiratorially.

KID, "In trouble already? I just came on shift!"

Betheny, "Oh KID, you know no one listens to the crazy old lady in the wheelchair. The old lady whose son pays three thousand dollars a month to keep locked up! You'd think the ' client ' would be shown more respect!" she throws the nurse's way.

The nurse fumes, spins around and charges down the hall.

Lester reads a text message, already bored.

"Why don't we go for a stroll around the grounds?" KID warmly suggests.

Betheny nods in approval as KID begins to wheel her outside.

Lester has been very busy since he wrestled away the power of attorney from his spiteful mother. Not wanting to leave anything to chance, he has been liquidating her considerable assets left right and center. Seems like her deceased husband, Winslow, thought the world of her and set her up nicely so money would never be a concern. Lester has really enjoyed the experience and has been strutting around like a barnyard rooster who has just satisfied the entire flock.

Who came first, indeed!

Except Lester doesn't think like that and really never had much interest in sex. At least sex with another person. Lester is an aficionada of the ' sex with alien ' porn genre and the more tentacles the better!

Lester has just put a sizable junk of property on the market and the offers are just pouring in. The old ' Animaland ' site off route 114, which is now overgrown with brush and weeds and quite the eyesore, is for sale.

He's never been one for art or artistic expression and buys most of his wall coverings and paintings from the same stores Betheny buys her clothes.

His father, Winslow, on the other hand, was quite famous in these parts and the sole artist and creator of ' Animaland ' which was a gift of love to his wife. She's always demanding to be taken on a field trip to visit the site but that would be such a chore that Lester flat out refuses.

And soon there will be no menagerie to visit.

Most folks around here would love to see it developed into a park or heritage site or anything else to draw tourists into the area. No one wants a subdivision or a new hotel - especially the owners of the ' Timberland Motel ' and the upscale ' Pine Cone '.

Who the hell do they think they are anyway with their fancy non-cinderblock rooms and WI fi?

I'll wipe that she she smirk off their faces when Travelodge or Holiday Inn Express makes me a tasty offer!

Betheny and KID enjoy their surroundings and the comfortable silence. They sit beside a hemlock tree whose long limbs wave along the ground like sea anemones in a gentle current. A few birds look for worms and seeds nearby and occasionally glance up at the strange couple who just smile and enjoy the day.

Betheny breaks the silence, "Did you bring my nerve medicine?"

KID laughs, at their private joke, and pulls out a tightly rolled joint awaiting inspection.

"Good thing too as you are acting especially nervous today!" he chuckles.

"I need a toot after dealing with jackass!" she spits, "I know he's up to something! He never spends more than ten minutes with me and as far as I know he's still here!"

KID lights up, takes a long practiced toke and passes the joint to Betheny who takes an equally impressive drag.

She holds it in and exhales, "Ever hear of shitbelly?"

KID cocks his head, "You mean like Elvis Shit Belly Presley?"

"So, it's a real thing?" she asks.

"Damn straight!" KID replies.

And that's the extent of their conversation as they reduce the joint to ash and while away the rest of the afternoon in mellow bliss.

The ' Animaland ' site is abuzz with worker bees busily completing their function for the greater good of the hive. A survey crew takes their measurements and hammer in orange tipped stakes for future reference, turning the sprawling acreage into a more manageable grid.

Lester strolls along with Lisa and Gene who are in charge of development at Holiday Inn Express.

Gene is thin and tall and lets Lisa do most of the talking. He wears jeans, tee and a vest and worn in hiking boots and from the look of them – they're made of Gore-Tex.

Bastard must make a bundle!

Lisa is thin as well and has a pretty good ass but her healthy pink skin is doing nothing for Lester's alien sex fantasizing. She wears one of those ' I'd have a huge penis if I was a man ' woman's business suits and high heels.

"What a moron!" Lester thinks as he listens to the ' suck ' noise Lisa's heels make as they sink into the muddy ground.

The moron wearing the heels stops and stares at Lester.

"Sorry, didn't catch that?" Lisa asks.

"Sorry?" Lester apologetically quips; realizing his inside voice was momentarily outside.

Lisa scowls, "When can we get the bulldozers in here?"

Lester, "Well the ground is a bit too soft for that but I'd say a few days."

She nods and grimaces when she notices the odd looking concrete spider sitting inert in an overgrown clearing.

She points, "And can we get that crap disposed of? They give me the creeps!"

Lester grins knowing that those creep-giving creatures are actually artworks created by his father and his opinion of Lisa goes up one notch

"They're not everyone's cup of tea, that's for sure." Lester jokes, "I'll see what I can do but after Friday, this is all yours."

He spreads his arms wide and pivots three hundred and sixty degrees.

"HE DID WHAT?" Betheny shrieks when she hears that her beloved, ' Animaland ', created by her beloved, has been sold to developers.

The news has been conveyed via Jerome, the local heavy-equipment operator and the one who will do the bulldozing. Jerome wears work clothes twenty- four-seven and Bethany often wondered if ' Dickies ' made formal wear? What does he wear at funerals and weddings? He and Winslow were good pals and it's out of a sense of decency and loyalty that Jerome has come in person.

Jerome sheepishly gazes at his feet, "I'm sorry Betheny. I feel like a real heal to be the one that has to scrape it clean but I didn't want you to hear it from a gossip or the media."

Betheny clasps his hand in hers and pats it, "Don't you fret Jerome, you're just doing your job and a man's got to earn a living." she smiles up at him, "Now, how long have I got before you start work?"

"Soon as the earth dries out, it's a helluva muddy mess out there right now." he replies.

"A bit of time then." Betheny whispers to herself.

Lester taps the bell, on the counter of the functional but ugly nurse's station, with one bony finger. He's startled by how loud it sounds in the now quiet seniors residence. All the inmates have now gone to bed. He looks at the brand new Tagheuer watch he just bought himself and smiles at how good it looks and how much it cost and that the hour is only eight pm. All the old men and women begin to fade with the sunlight. Why this might even be the last night on earth for some of them. He doubts his mother will be one of them.

No, she'll linger just to spite me!

One of the nurses comes barreling out from the nurse's inner sanctum, an aggressive scowl on her face expecting a troublesome inmate. The scowl softens a bit when she sees Lester and gets tinged with curiosity at the intrusion and at such a relatively late hour.

"Visiting hours are over! Can I help you with something?" she grills inquisitor like.

Lester gives her the stink-eye as his mother was correct in stating that he did pay three thousand dollars a month to keep her wheelchair bound ass in captivity.

"My Mother isn't in her room, her beds not slept in," Lester points out.

"Well, she's gotta be here, we've never lost anyone!" the nurse brags.

"Until now!" Lester emphasizes.

The nurse, sensing that Lester won't be placated, sighs and heads off in the direction of Betheny's room, cursing her luck under her breath,

Lester watches her fume as she stamps away like an eight-year-old who wanted cotton candy ice cream and got vanilla instead. He decides to make the most out of his mother's disappearance. He will ring the bell every minute until his mother is found or he has emptied out the nurse's station.

He pounds on the bell, with the heal of his hand, and another annoyed nurse charges out to challenge him. But before she can speak, he goes on the offensive, "My mother is not in her room and presumed missing."

The new nurse stares at him quizzically and off-balance, "Didn't another nurse come out to assist you?"

"Why no." Lester dead pans, "Don't tell me you've lost a nurse as well! Just what kind of facility are you attempting to run here?"

The new nurse scans up and down the hallway, as if the act will suddenly materialize the missing nurse and Lester's mother.

The orange-yellow sun hangs low over the horizon and reflects off the chipping paint of the ancient seniors residence mobility van.

"Immobility van!" jokes Betheny as the elevated ramp whirs and strains to gently deposit her on the muddy ground. KID works the hydraulics with practiced efficiency and non-chalance. His usual cool and collected demeanor is tarnished with the unease of expectation. The expectation that something is too easy and getting caught is imminent. The lift suddenly drops the last inch and makes a splat sound when it displaces the mud. KID races over to Betheny to make sure she is okay.

"Break anything?" KID asks.

"Just what's left of my pride! I may have peed a little when the lift lurched!" Betheny chuckles.

"No big deal my friend." KID shoots back.

Betheny studies KID with fondness as he frees the wheelchair from the safety straps.

"Is that what we are? Friends?" Betheny asks.

KID works on the straps, "Must be cuz when they find out I sprung you from the home, I'll be looking for a new job or maybe jail time!"

Betheny laughs, "It won't come to that. I'll take care of you."

KID steps back, hand on hips, "How the hell you gonna do that?"

She grins broadly and calmly says, "You'd be surprised. You'd be surprised."

Lester flies down route 114 in his $ 70,000 Jeep Cherokee with the car stereo turned up. He likes to listen to 80's synth hits and right now he's driving to Blue Monday.

"Tell me how does it feel?" he howls out of tune.

Lester wonders how it would feel to throttle his mother for making him come out on such a crappy day to look for her. The morons at the home didn't even know she was missing but he has a pretty good idea where she's gone. His mother is as helpless as an ant under a child's magnifying glass. Mr. Goody Two Shoes, from the home, must have sprung her! He probably loves her more than Lester does which really isn't saying much as the old bat can be insufferable.

"He kind of looks native." Lester muses, "MicMac perhaps? Cherokee? Maybe he knows my Jeep?"

Lester careens into the weed-choked parking lot of ' Animaland ', mud projecting from the tires in fountains. The sun is just setting and it's dim and gloomy already.

He cuts the engine and steps out of the muddied Jeep - named after a First Nations people. His brown dress shoes sink into the brown mud, happy to blend in for a change.

Lester on the other hand curses his luck, "That's just great!"

He fumbles in his jacket pocket and produces a small blue dollar-store flashlight, turns it on and scans the parking lot. Empty with the exception of the mobility van whose wheelchair elevator platform rests on the mucky ground.

Lester, much like his flashlight, beams and says. "Got you now!"

KID grunts and groans as he tries to push the wheelchair through the quagmire of the once manicured ' Animaland ' grounds. He comes to a soggy halt and leans on the wheelchair handles, doubling over to catch his breath. It's been years since he worked his body in such a way. He's reminded just what kind of training regiment he'd have to follow to play rugby again.

He gasps, "Can't go on! Too much mud."

Betheny, perched in her wheelchair high and dry, smiles and chuckles, "Oh, that's okay KID, we've gone far enough."

On her lap sits a white five-gallon plastic pail. KID, finally getting some air again, regards the bucket as if seeing it for the first time.

"Why'd you bring the bucket?"

"It's an essential part of our nocturnal adventure!" hints Betheny.

"Okay." KID plays along, "And what's all the rope for, in said bucket?"

"Leverage my friend! A pulley system takes less physical excursion and I'm old and lazy!" she chides him.

KID shakes his head and sarcastically says, "Whatever!"

Some unseen animal like a raccoon or porcupine rustles close by and engages KID's attention. He uses his limited human night vision to peer into the brush and identify the critter,

"Can't see shit but I'll bet it's a coyote!" KID brags.

KID feels warm even breathing on the back of his neck! You would think the warmth might block the, prickly back of the neck heebie jeebies, but it doesn't! Before he can slowly turn around to face the source of the breathing, he hears Betheny's voice as if she was the source, impossible as that might be.

"You forgot to ask me what the hammer was for?" she teases.

KID turns completely around and is shocked and mystified when he sees that wheelchair-bound Betheny is standing tall and straight in front of him.

She grins like an alligator with a swamp persons shotgun between it's formidable rows of razor-sharp teeth.

KID can only manage, "What?" and "How?" as his oxygen-starved brain tries to make sense of the sight before him.

And of course when his brain does fully recover and posturize what comes next – it's too late!

Betheny guides the brand new gleaming hammer, with the 'Home Hardware ' sticker still attached, in a rainbow like arc down and into KID's forehead and into the thickest part of the skull. The brand new hammer sinks into KID's grey matter and Bethany's only true friend slumps to the ground quite unconscious and quite possibly dead!

Lester stares down at his ruined brown dress shoes, illuminated by his cheap dollar store flashlight. He ponders whether to continue to search for his mother? His shoes won't recover so let the authorities take care of business while he heads home and has a hot shower. His pondering is interrupted by the sound, a brand new hammer might make, as it crunches down on a human skull.

"Probably just a branch snapping!" Lester says aloud and swallows making his overly large Adam's apple bob up and down.

His shoes forgotten, Lester swings the flashlight to and fro trying to catch a glimpse of the creature that broke the twig. He hopes it's a raccoon or something that size and definitely nothing bigger. He swallows, feeling a little unnerved and shivers making his shitbelly quiver.

KID, unconscious and secured around the ankles by a strong rope, hangs upside down from a sturdy tree branch. The five-gallon bucket sits on the muddy ground just below his head and his head sways ever so slightly - keeping time to his heartbeat as the blood rushes downward.

Betheny carefully creates a stone circle on the ground that's about three meters in diameter. She uses the rocks and pebbles she finds on the ground, choosing the worthy and discarding the rest and all the while she chants and chants quite happily.

The chant has no English translation but could be mistaken for Latin - if one had an ear for such things. Or perhaps the Latin language evolved from this root? Although the chanting is originating from Betheny's vocal chords, the sound seems to swirl around the stone circle. It takes on multiple tones as if being chanted by a multitude of entities. Some of the sounds do not emanate from human vocal chords and might be considered to be demonic in nature - according to horror movie depictions.

(And really, why would they lie?)

Poor Lester, by now, quite shaken and leaning towards getting in his gas-guzzling jeep *(of appropriation)* and running away.

(And there is absolutely no shame in running away! Men and women in the military have been doing it for thousands of years. But instead of running away they have coined the term ' retreating '!)

So, like proud military men and women from all over the world, Lester turns tail and as quickly as he can and retreats to his mud-covered vehicle. He climbs in and slams the door behind him. For the moment, he doesn't even care that the bill for cleaning and detailing his car will be through the roof. He's about to turn the engine over when he, just barely, hears what he thinks must be music coming from the woods. And in the same direction as the tree branch snap. The tiny motor, in his door panel, whirs and the window rolls down. And as it rolls down - the sound rises in volume.

Not music! Chanting!

Lester closes his eyes to concentrate on the sound and sighs. The chanting, he finds, is very comforting and also alluring and before he realizes what he is doing - he opens the door and gets out of the Jeep.

Whatever that sound is – I must find it! Lester decides.

Like a rodent entranced by a King Cobra, he is drawn into the woods, the door to his Jeep left wide open.

KID hangs like a deer in a hunter's garage. His throat has been jaggedly cut and the blood, that once sustained him, has filled the bucket to the brim. As the sun sets, the blood steams in the falling temperature.

Betheny places the last rock, in her very impressive and improvised circle, stands up tall and smiles and nods at a job well done. Her muddy and soiled clothes form a lumpy pile near the slightly swaying and non-slightly dead, KID. Betheny sighs remorsefully thinking what cold have been and gazes lovingly at her friend.

"Sorry KID! This wasn't the end for you I had envisioned but my disappointment of a son, forced my hand. I hope you lived a good life and I sure enjoyed our time together. Good bye my friend and I will see you in the light far away from this heavy planet." Betheny eulogizes and even waves goodbye.

Sentimental fool!

She chuckles then kneels beside the bucket and begins to smudge herself.

(But not a smudge with dried sage or sweet grass as one might say ' normal people ' do. The truth is that most of the residents of the province and most of Canada, for that matter, don't even know what smudging is. If they've heard of it, they probably associate it with four-twenty dirty-hippies! Most likely from Vancouver!)

Betheny's people, however, have always used blood and she works it into her skin as she cleanses herself. She gives thanks to the four directions, the earth and the sky and her ancestors and of course her friend, KID.

Lester tromps through the bush, the anti-thesis of a skilled and stealthy tracker.

If, by chance, someone had concealed a whoppie-cushion in the woods, Lester would have stepped on it. He stops for a moment, stepping on and snapping yet another dry twig, and cocks his head to listen to the forest and the chanting that stopped long ago. An odd sound to his left – an out of place sound. It's almost like the sound a tied-off boat makes as the wave motion makes it rise and fall and strain to be set free. Free on the open water where boats are supposed to be. But there's no ocean close by nor is there a lake or river for that matter! Intrigued, Lester cautiously creeps through the trees in the direction of…. creaking!

That's the sound! It is a rope and it's creaking just like a boat.

Lester excitedly quickens his pace and of course his noise footprint is magnified ten-fold.

(Imagine a rhino charging through a balsa wood airplane factory and you get the idea!)

A gnarled root has the misfortune of meeting Lester's muddy foot which sends Lester diving forward, out of control, and heading for the wet but still hard earth.

He's moving so fast that he falls out of the brush and into a clearing where he slams into the earth with bone-wrenching force and in this case - shitbelly squishing force! Dazed, and his breath knocked out of him, Lester lies in a heap. He keeps his eyes closed as he waits for the pain to pass and he hopes that it will, in fact, pass soon.

Betheny caresses some of the blood, from her bucket, into the antennae of a giant red cement lobster. The lobster was once used as a children's slide, and as she works, Bethany begins to chant once again. Almost immediately, the antennae begin to twitch and respond to her touch. She laughs and continues to smudge the lobster from head to toe or in this case antenna to tail. When she's finished she stands back to admire her work.

She smiles and utters one last chant, which translates into something like, "Arise old one, arise and live again!"

And that's just what happens as the giant red lobster comes to life! When the eyes on the ends of it's giant antenna stocks see Betheny, it wags its giant red lobster tail like a dog whose master has just stepped in the door after a long absence.

Betheny moves in close and strokes the lobster's head, "I missed you too!"

With the bucket of blood held firm by her inner thigh muscles, naked Betheny sits atop the re-animated lobster as if she were riding an elephant. Not considered a silent hunter, like a jaguar or a snake, the lobster makes considerable noise as it scuttles through the park. It crashes through the undergrowth, leaving a large wake where it has passed. Betheny is having a grand time and they frequently stop to make more re-animations. Coming back to life are a giant spider, an elephant and a rather macabre skeletal and misshapen giant mule. The mule looking like it trotted out of a ghoulish nightmare rather than a tourist attraction.

Lester finally opens his eyes; feeling like the worst of the pain has passed. He has become aware of a thunderous crashing - making the earth shake in the nearby woods.

"Tyrannosaurus Rex?" Lester muses to himself, "That was a fun movie, Jurassic Park!"

Of course, Lester didn't pay almost twenty bucks to go to a proper theatre and see the film where it was designed to be seen. No, he illegally downloaded it and watched it on his IPhone.

(That's right he stole it, plain and simple!
What would David Lynch say of such practices!)

The creaking sound draws Lester's attention and he takes stock of his surroundings. A clearing of sorts, as everything is over grown with weeds, and what looks like a stone circle and a bag tied up in a tree. Lester gets up slowly and tries to dust himself off. Since all the dust is quite damp, he accidentally smears mud all over his clothes. He looks back at the bag hanging in the tree and realizes, too late, that the bag is, in fact, the exsanguinated body of that troublesome do-gooder from the home! Bile, followed by quite a bit of vomit, has raced up and out of Lester's throat, past his unusually large Adam's apple and splashed onto the muddy and bloody earth and his once pristine shoes.

The cement menagerie closes in on Lester's location and they advance toward the clearing from every direction. Leading the advance is Betheny. She its astride the mule, with it's odd proportions and emaciated body, looking very much like one of the four horsemen *(or women)* of the apocalypse.

Poor Lester, so preoccupied with puking, doesn't hear their approach and it's quite easy for the mule to sneak up and butt Lester forward into his own massive puke pile!

Lester holds up his hands now covered in vomit, blood and mud, "Disgusting!" he shoots to his feet and screams, "WHAT THE HELL?"

The feistiness almost leaves Lester's body, as fast as his stomach contents when he spins around to see Betheny. She smiles at him and her band of concrete animals stares right through him. He doesn't believe for one moment that these ' shitty eye sores ', someone deemed art, could actually come to life so he uses his hands to wipe his eyes and hopefully clear his vision. Unfortunately for Lester, on this unfortunate night, the very same hands he used to wipe his eyes are the very same hands covered in blood, mud, vomit and quite possible dog shit. The locals have been bringing their dogs here for years and using it as an unofficial off-leash park.

Lester let's out a yelp. His eyes not only sting but feel like they are on fire! Which could very well be. Betheny infused KID's blood with magic when she was chanting and perhaps it wasn't the good kind of magic that unicorn riding wizards might conjure up. Perhaps it was more akin to the demonic blood ritual magic that world and business leaders undergo at Bohemian Grove?

Runny blood, mud, vomit and dog-shit now stream down Lester's face mixed with his tears. He moans and sobs quietly to himself waiting for his vision to clear.

"This just gets better and better!" Betheny laughs from high up on the mule "Stop your blubbering!"

"Mother?" Lester asks, waving his hands about like a birthday boy reaching for the piñata.

"Over here Shitbelly!" Betheny taunts from atop the mule.

"I can't see a thing!" Lester whines, "I think I'm blind."

"Maybe just as well. You never had much of an appreciation for art or anything worthwhile. `. Betheny snorts.

Lester hones in on the sound of her voice and begins to cautiously take one sloppy footstep at a time, hands held out in front of him to feel his way along.

"You sold Animaland behind my back, you cowardly little troll! How could you do that? You knew that was Winslow's gift to me! It should have been classified a heritage site and refurbished." says Betheny.

Lester has picked up speed somewhat, getting the gist of this, walking through quicksand and blinded by blood, mud, vomit, tears and dog-shit, routine.

In fact, he's feeling much more like the rooster and remembers who and how insignificant this person, his mother, is!

He shoots back, "It's an overgrown eye-sore of poorly cast concrete and quite ugly play ground toys. Amateurish at best and quite creepy!"

"Your father didn't create them, you idiot!" Betheny snaps back, "Winslow just secured the land for me. They're not made of concrete either; they're made from clay. A very special clay that can only be found in this province and in particular, this tract of land. You're standing on a gold mine and you just sold it!"

Lester frowns, "No, I had the property appraised! There's nothing here worth any money!"

"Oh, it's more valuable than gold or silver." Betheny smirks, "when molded from the right hands."

"What?" Lester says in frustration and just then one of his waving hands comes in contact with a solid warm object that seems to be covered in coarse hair.

Betheny smiles as she watches her son grope the muzzle of her skeletal stead.

He feels and caresses the length of it being gentle at first then getting rougher,

"What the hell is this...?" Lester asks but before he can say ' thing ' he jabs the muzzle with two bony fingers, making the mule wince.

In a purely reflexive reaction, the macabre mule bites down hard on the nearest part of Lester - crunching down on Lester's forearm. Like the snapping twigs that intrigued KID and then Lester earlier this evening, the ulna and radius bones in poor Lester's arm, snap in two. Lester cries out in agony as the mule, no longer in reflex mode, gives Lester's arm a good shake before letting him go.

The mule's eyes that were previously a chestnut brown now burn with glowing fire and it's nostrils flare and snort as it stamps the muddy ground with it's massive hooves. Lester's agonized screams have catalyzed the other creatures as well and they all move about in agitated anticipation of what's to come.

(It's as if they know already!)

Lester staggers back, whimpering and holding up his almost severed arm. His hand and wrist, daggle limply, and quite grotesquely.

Invisibly and wordlessly, Betheny signals the menagerie to close the circle even further.

Lester appears to be on the verge of passing out but just before his legs buckle, the mule uses his formidable muzzle to send Lester sprawling into the center of the re-animated creatures.

Lester finds his voice once more. This new voice however is not that of the crowing rooster who so proudly boasted how he was taking his wheelchair-bound mother to the cleaners. No, this is the quivering cry of a sleepy child woken up by the horrifying visions of a nightmare. Thankfully, this man-child cannot see the horrifying visions that surround him right now. And as a result, his already over taxed brain does not have to make sense of such a sight.

"You won't get away with this! I'll charge you with assault and bodily harm. I'll get you assessed and thrown in a psych ward for the rest of your miserable life. You thought the home was bad? That will seem like a freakin holiday!" Lester pouts.

"You'll do nothing of the sort!" Betheny warns Lester. "Now stand up and face the consequences of your actions."

"Consequences for what?" Lester wonders aloud.

"Putting your ill mother in a home for one! Going behind my back and liquidating my assets for another! And for being a lousy son in general! Mothers are supposed to be proud of their children! We need something to brag about to one another!" Betheny explains.

Lester throws his hands up in the air, *(only one really)*, in exasperation, "Well I'm so sorry I'm such a disappointment!"

"Oh, I don't believe you are. But you will be soon!" Betheny sings.

Lester's tear ducts, working overtime, have finally succeeded in getting most of the blood, mud, vomit and dog-shit from Lester's eyes and he begins to see again, but not clearly. He seems to be surrounded by giants. What kind of giants he can't yet tell.

Perhaps they could be trees?
Fence posts?
Light standards?
Very large rocks?
Wait a minute, are they moving?
Trees then!
Very oddly shaped trees like giant hedge animals!

Lester actually smiles, proud of himself for figuring things out.

"Now, who wants to take care of Shitbelly?" Betheny quizzes the menagerie.

They all stamp their feet and shake their tails, or their bodies, if they don't have tails. The giant spider holds up one of his eight legs, like a smart kid in a schoolroom who desperately knows the answer - but the teacher is ignoring. The massive elephant trumpets vigorously but no sound comes out of her clay trunk. The huge lobster wags her formidable tail, dog-like, and the gaunt mule rears up on his hind legs trying to win Betheny's favor. Betheny laughs heartily, touched by the enthusiasm of her blood magic creations.

"Now, don't fret, everyone will get a turn and if I don't pick you this time, don't sulk." Betheny re-assures her charges.

She looks around, pausing for a few moments, on each creature - silently weighing their merits.

"Lester, do you like lobster?" Betheny asks.

"Well, ya! Who doesn't?" he snorts back.

"Good." Betheny beams, "I'm sure she'll like you too!"

The giant lobster is beside herself, in excitement, and slaps her elongated tail on the muddy ground. The others are rather dejected even though Betheny is always true to her word and deep down inside - they know they will get their chance. The mule scuffs the dirt and snorts. The spider rolls over on it's back and plays dead.

The elephant sucks on it's trunk like a pacifier.

"What?" is all Lester can muster.

All of a sudden he's feeling exhausted. He doesn't get much exercise, as his shitbelly would attest, although he does get his heart rate up when he's indulging in has special brand of porn. But right now, he is done in and just wants to go home and lick his wounds. Speaking of which, he should also stop at the hospital to see if they can get his arm in working order.

"I need medical attention! I need it NOW!" Lester shouts at his mother.

"You don't need a doctor you big baby! You need a priest!" Betheny teases.

"A priest? What the hell are you on about now, ya old bat!" Lester throws back confused.

"Any last words, Shitbelly!" Betheny prompts and signals the monstrous red lobster to proceed at any time.

The lobster slowly scuttles toward Lester, enjoying each step.

Her fellow creatures have ceased their childish resentments and all eyes are now focused on the spectacle enfolding with delicious slowness.

Lester senses a change in the air and cocks his head in an attempt to discern what the clicking sound is and what's making the earth shake and rumble.

The lobster closes in on poor Lester who can't clearly see what 's coming for him. She begins to click her massive claws, open and closed, which makes the sound of two large pieces of fiberglass being struck with a sledgehammer. She halts her forward progress, savoring the moment.

Silence ensues! Not even a rodent rustles the grass; this moment seems frozen in time,

Lester's equilibrium falters, from the lack of sound, and he almost falls to one knee.

"Mother?" Lester cries.

Instead of answering and re-assuring her only son, Betheny grins even more broadly and has to suck in some spittle that was running down the corners of her lips.

Oh my God! She thinks to herself, I'm *drooling!*

The lobster extends her open left claw and carefully positions it around Lester's body - waist height. She holds it there, poised, as Betheny and the rest of the blood magic creatures lean forward in anticipation. The claw begins to close slowly and surely like a giant crustacean vice until it meets flesh Lester cries out as the cerated edge of the claw digs into his back and belly. Blood begins to soak his very expensive shirt and pants. The lobster is taken aback as she was trying to be so very careful and gentle.

(But really, how gentle can a one-tonne clay monster really be?)

Her claw divides Lester's shitbelly in two, making it look like a strange figure eight shape.

Poor Lester coughs up blood and begins to feel light headed.

"Why, mother, why?" he croaks

Under her breath, Betheny quips, "Just die already!"

Sensing her plaything will soon become a dead thing, the lobster moves with more intent. With a speed one, wouldn't think possible from a magic giant clay lobster, she raises her right claw and in one deft motion, decapitates Lester. Blood springs straight up from his neck!

The menagerie is elated and show their appreciation with stomping, trumpeting and bucking. When she's not hanging on for dear life, Betheny claps and whistles.

Lester's bodiless head has somehow rolled across the muck and ended upright and facing the spectacle. The roll across the mud and water has cleared his vision giving him a front row seat, so to speak. He watches, in horror, as his body - splashes everything within a two-meter radius with his dark blood. He also notices that a rather large red lobster is now holding said body and that an elephant, spider and mule, carrying his mother, are having a delightful time watching his life force ebb away. And then thankfully for Lester, the remaining blood drains from his decapitated head and the topsy-turvy world fades out!

The blood fountain has stopped spurting so the lobster throws Lester's body into the bush and returns to her previous spot in the circle.

Betheny beams and says, "That was just wonderful! Thank you lobster."

The lobster being painted in Kid's red blood already - can hardly blush, but if she could - she would!

"Now, I believe dawn is coming and with the dawn comes opportunity.

I imagine the good folks, from Holiday Inn Express, and Jerome will be here bright and early with all the heavy equipment. So everyone will get their turn like I promised!" Betheny assures her troops.

They all dance and spin around showing their appreciation and love for their creator.

Betheny smiles and sighs a deep satisfied sigh, "Oh, Animaland – how I've missed you?"

The End.

GROUND ZERO

The Technician, slowly swims to the surface of consciousness. He's forty, brown-hair cut short, stubble with a few patches of grey and handsome in a nerdy pocket-protector way. He tries to focus on his private hospital room. All the equipment gleams and sparkles as if brand new and he studies his surroundings with eyes groggy from painkillers.

A female Doctor makes notes on an IPad. She's thirty-five, equine features, possible Egyptian ancestry, dressed in deep crimson scrubs and a deep crimson lab coat. A strained smile appears on her face as if her skin was stretched too tight and not used to elasticized movements.

"Welcome back", she offers.

The Technician scans the room, "Where am I?"

"In a grotesquely expensive private hospital - recovering from a brutal assault." she says matter-of-factly.

"Attack? Who?"

The Doctor looks at him curiously, "You don't remember?"

Technician, "Not a thing!"

The Doctor attempts a grin although it looks more like rictus, "Not such a bad thing."

The Technician tilts his head curiously, "Why would you say that?"

Doctor, "Are you in much pain?"

The Technician laughs, "I feel like I'm wasted."

She laughs, "Morphine."

The Technician frowns, "Sounds bad."

Doctor, "The phrase lucky to be alive comes to mind."

The Technician glares, "Who did this?"

The Doctor sighs, "We'll get to that. But for now it's time for you to dive into the deep end!"

She reaches over and opens the morphine drip as wide as it will go, then smiles sort of. In a few seconds the Technician passes out and passes out pleasurably.

She then taps a tiny polished steel disc seated in her left ear canal, "Yes. He claims he doesn't remember a thing. Could be post-traumatic amnesia."

She taps the disc again and is about to leave when she notices that the intravenous on the back of his hand is encircled by a bloody scab. She sighs as she falls on the scab; a ravenous beast, devouring the crust and licking the wound clean with her snaking tongue.

In a dim minimalist boardroom, a meeting is underway. The center of the room is weighed down with a massive black marble table surrounded by blood red chairs. The floor, also black marble, gleams and reflects the flickering candles from the ornate silver sconces on the walls. Also reflecting the candlelight are the yellow serpentine eyes of three people seated at the table.

The Doctor sits, resplendent, in a black stretchy dress that clings to her lithe body like a second skin. Embedded in the pale skin between her eyes is a small red bindy. The circle has a black background and a sigil of her tribe – Saturn before the rings

Opposite the Doctor, is Luka, a black male of considerable stature. He looks as if he is chiseled from the same marble as the table and similarly animated. He wears a black sleeveless PVC shirt and black combat pants tucked into black Doc Martins. His thick charcoal hair is braided into short dreads and shaved on the sides and back. He also dons the same sigil as the Doctor but his is tattooed on his muscular right bicep.

Sitting at the head of the table is Romaine. A heavy-set Slavic looking man with a close-cropped beard and conservative haircut. His dress is also conservative in nature with a black sport coat and black tee shirt, and black slacks. On his left middle finger gleams a surgical steel ring with the same sigil as the others.

Romaine gets the meeting started with his commanding booming voice, "What of our Environmental Protection Act approval next week?"

Luka waves a dismissive hand, "Not a problem, we have the Minister firmly secured in our back pocket. Consider the waste-water berm approved."

Romaine nods and grins which allow his sharp alabaster canines to peek out, "Any opposition?"

Luka shrugs, "Sporadic at best. The usual First Nations posturing."

Romaine chuckles, "In other words, no one cares!"

Romaine and Luka turn their gaze to the Doctor.

Romaine, "And what of the man who knew too much?"

Serenely, the Doctor says, "Recovering, but he remembers nothing. He may never regain those memories which I firmly believe are repressed and not a result of physical damage."

Romaine, "Options?"

The Doctor nods, "One, we monitor his recovery and hope the memories remain locked away. Two, we turn him. Three, we kill him. Four, we recruit him and read him in."

They all chuckle delightedly.

Luka jokes, "A new Renfield!"

Doctor, "Why not!"

Luka and Romaine in unison, "Why not!"

The Doctor stands, statuesque, at the foot of the Technicians hospital bed and wills him to consciousness. He slowly comes around and takes a few moments to focus on the Doctor and smiles.

Technician hopefully, "Good news?"

The Doctor coldly, "That's not up to me."

The Technician frowns, "That's an odd thing to say. What an odd bedside manner you have."

The Doctor breaks a smile, "It's more along the lines of a proposition."

The Technician makes encouraging hand signals.

The Doctor continues, "What if I had the means to make you even better than you were before the assault?"

The Technician spits, "I'd say you must be under the thumb of big Pharma and want to include me in a new untested drug trial."

The Doctor chuckles, "No, nothing vulgar like that. My methods are tried and true, tested over centuries."

The Technician looks at her quizzically, "Sounds too good to be true! What do I have to do?"

"Work for me and my colleagues on a top secret project." she says candidly.

He laughs, "Is that all? How do you know I'm trustworthy?"

Doctor, "I just have a feeling."

Technician, "Anything else?"

Doctor, "Just one more thing."

Technician, "And what's that?"

Doctor, "You have to die!"

Two weeks later, the Technician, still badly bruised and wearing a neck brace, sits at the conference room table with Luka and Romaine as the Doctor runs though a multimedia presentation. The Doctor advances a slide depicting a cross-section of bitumen and in the middle of the slide, a small red circle.

The Doctor explains, 'When our engineers first evaluated the potential of the sands they found this."

The image magnifies and inside the red circle is a small fetus.

The Technician, "Is that an embryo?"

Romaine, "It is indeed!"

The Technician, "But what's it doing in the tar?"

Luka, "No one knew until just recently."

Doctor, "In the Ceriozoic era we know that many species of hominids were competing to survive and out of that competition, modern-day Homo sapiens would appear. But there was one species no one knew about until the tar sands were developed."

The Technician leans forward, "A new species? This is amazing!"

Luka grins, "Oh, it gets better!"

Romaine laughs, "Much better!"

The Doctor grins, "I don't know if you're ready for it. But you need to see it for yourself!"

She clicks a remote and a CCTV feed begins to play on the screen. The video reveals a wide shot of the Technician in his state of the art laboratory. He works at a tall steel counter dressed in a lab coat and assisted by two young and good looking female assistants. They joke and flirt as they label and catalogue many test tubes filled with viscous black sludge. The Technician tries to impress the assistants by balancing a beaker on one latex-gloved index finger. The beaker begins to teeter in every direction then falls to the counter-top careening into numerous test tubes and sending shards of glass and debris in all directions. The momentum of the Technician's hand slams it down on the jagged shards and he screams in pain. He holds up his mutilated hand, dripping blood onto the spreading lava of bitumen. The sludge begins to bubble and the Technician and assistants back away in fear.

The screen fills with static, for a millisecond, and when it clears - we see a huge hulking shape tearing the head off one of the assistants like a cork from a champagne bottle. With super human strength, the creature turns the body upside down and guzzles the cascade of hot blood still pumping out of the assistant's neck.

Another wave of static then back to the laboratory just in time to see the Technician fly through the air and smash against the far wall, hurled by the creature. The other assistant lies drained and lifeless, draped awkwardly over the steel counter. The creature turns and roars at the camera, somehow aware of the camera's presence. The creature is the size of an All Blacks rugby player. It's hairless with grey scaly skin, deep set crimson eyes, a pit-bull like jaw structure and cruel long teeth with very pronounced fangs.

A red tranquilizer dart slams into the creature's temple. The creature barely feels it and brushes it away like a gnat. Someone off camera attracts the creature's attention and it turns toward the source of the annoying darts and roars defiantly. Darts of all colors pepper the creatures face and neck. The creature remains solidly in place but begins to drool. Four dart gun-totting SWAT team figures, with the same Saturn before the rings sigils, surround the creature and manage to wrestle it to the floor and immobilize it.

The Doctor presses a button on the remote and the screen fades to black. The Technician sits back into his chair, eyes wide and mouth hanging open. His eyes flicker from the Doctor to Luka and Romaine then roll up into his head and he faints.

The Technician comes to sputtering and choking as the Doctor waves smelling salts under his nose.

When he calms down, tears flow down his bruised cheeks and he pleads, '"That really happened? Tell me it was CGI or a dream!"

The Doctor looks at him sympathetically while Luka and Romaine can barely contain their mirth.

Doctor, "You know it wasn't a dream!"

The Technician sighs, "What was that thing?"

Romaine rises majestically and takes over the presentation from the Doctor, "One of us I'm afraid, in our most primitive state!"

He clicks the remote and a slide of the unconscious creature, lying on an operating table. fills the screen.

He continues, "Who knew a few drops of blood could resuscitate the ancestors!"

The Technician cocks his head quizzically, "Your ancestors and not mine!"

Romaine, "Correct."

Technician, "And you are?"

Romaine, "We're humanoid. We just evolved on a different dietary path. While you are a generalist, we are specialized much like a Koala Bear and eucalyptus leaves."

Luka pipes up devouring the Technician with his eyes, "Blood is all our kind requires. Hot steaming human blood!"

Romaine scolds him, "ENOUGH!"

Technician, "Vampires!"

Romaine makes an attempt at a smile, "We prefer Saguinus Nocturna."

The Technician spits, "A rose by any other name." he studies the vampires, "Why are you and that creature so different?"

The Doctor grins, "Why are you and Neanderthals so different?"

The Technician quips, 'Touché." he evaluates them, "Why am I still alive? I know too much."

Doctor, "We'd like you to keep working for us and with us. You possess a skill set we find desirable and you are immune to the suns rays."

The Technician, "And just what is it that you think I can do for you?"

Romaine, "You can be our media and government liaison and of course you can continue your research."

Technician, "Do I get a raise?"

Everyone laughs.

Technician, "So, You're tripling my workload but I'm not seeing any carrot!"

The Doctor takes the remote from Romaine and clicks on a slide of numerous brain scans which all clearly show a tennis ball-sized white mass.

Solemnly the Doctor reports, "These were all taken just after the attack. The trauma inflicted by said attack has resulted in a tumor."

Technician, "Jesus, it's huge!"
The Doctor, "And unfortunately quite fatal."
Technician calmly, "How long?"
Doctor, "Twelve months optimistically."
The Technician blows air through his lips,
"There's is nothing optimistic about this situation."
Tears, well in his eyes, and cascade down his
cheeks. After a considerate amount of time,
Romaine glides over to the Technician and stands
stolidly in front of him.
With surprising compassion he says, "In your
world this is a death sentence. In my world it is not!
Disease, damage, and aging – they don't exist. Our
work here is almost complete and all we need is
one year to accomplish our goals. You coincidently
have one year and then…"
Luka, "A choice."
Doctor, "A reward."
Romaine, "A gift! And considering you know
too much – that is the penultimate carrot!"
The Technician takes his time, leans back in his
chair confidently and says, "Tell me everything so I
can make a more informed decision."
The vampires laugh delightedly.
Luka booms, "You have no bargaining power!
Either you die a year from now or tonight!"
Romaine smiles in a fatherly manner, "What my
younger colleague means is that we would like or
prefer for you to work with us and join us of your
own volition rather than exsanguinate you on the
spot."
The Technician slowly gets up and wanders
over to the vast window that overlooks the Tar
Sands. The nighttime view is stark and desolate.

The scraped, gouged and raped earth as far as the eyes can see. The floodlights cast grotesque misshapen shadows on the nightmarish landscape.

Romaine joins the Technician and sweeps a gesturing arm toward the view.

He asks, "What does it remind you of?"

The Technician ponders thoughtfully then replies, "I'm torn between Dante's Inferno and Mordor,"

Romaine glares at the Technician, "It reminds me of home. A light devouring void of desolation. Our ground zero. Our Bikini Atoll,"

The Technician raises his eyebrows, "What are you testing?"

Romaine, "How long it will take to terraform this sunny and verdant world."

The Technician spins to the floor like a burning spitfire over London. He sits with his legs folded underneath him and uses his hands to steady himself.

Doctor, "Alright?"

Technician, "Dizzy."

Doctor, "These spells will become more frequent with time."

Luka stands and leans against the desk, arms folded, "In time we will daywalk as the haze of burning fossil fuel blots out the sun. Photosynthesis will no longer work."

The Technician, "My kind will starve."

Luka, " We're only interested in keeping and maintaining the infrastructure of your cities. We can use them for food maintenance and storage. "

Technician, "What's with the pipeline push? Why is that so important?'

Romaine explains, "The embryo found in the bitumen. It's too time intensive and labor intensive to locate them in the oil. So we decided on an alternative distribution method,"

Technician, "Aerial dispersion?"

Romaine shakes his head, "Too obvious! How does one get oil into the environment?"

Technician "Spills."

Romaine smiles, "Exactly! Our pipelines are really quite safe and indestructible."

The Technician frowns, "But spills happen all the time. That's why you're feeling the heat in BC."

Luka laughs, "And so?"

The Technician ponders a moment then responds, 'They're intentional!"

Romaine crows, "They're all intentional! Accelerating the terraforming required drastic measures."

The Technician frowns, "But how does this help with resuscitating your kind?"

The Doctor joins in, "As you proved in the lab, all that it takes is a single drop of blood."

Technician, "But my blood was in a small confined space! How will you trigger the embryo's?"

The Doctor smiles slyly, "You humans are everywhere and you're constantly shedding blood, accidently and with your meaningless wars and invasions!"

All the vampires grin.

Technician, "I still don't understand why you need the creatures?"

Luka, "As I mentioned, we aren't interested in the rural communities. The ancestors will eradicate any possible human resistance by eradicating any rural population. There is ample sustenance in the cities to sustain us indefinitely."

The Technician shakes his head, "But surely someone will stop you. Someone will find you out. The military, the government. What about the PM? Isn't he a tree-hugger?"

Doctor reassuringly, "Oh, we turned him at the same time we turned his father! There is no one left to stop us. Anyone that could is one of us."

Luka, " Or has been eaten by one of us."

Romaine, "Ready to earn your immortality?"

The Technician spits, "Like I have a choice "

Luka, "We all have choices. You could die a horrible natural death."

The Technician sighs, "What do you want me to do?"

Romaine rubs his hands together in anticipation, "We want you to create and plant a glowing news story about a new pipeline. The usual drivel about job creation, the economy..."

The End.

274

www.cmhindmarshbooks.com